Sweet Little Lies

ABBI GLINES

#1 *NEW YORK TIMES* BESTSELLING AUTHOR

Sweet Little Lies
Copyright © 2017 by Abbi Glines

Published by
Abbi Glines
10 N Section Street
Suite 147
Fairhope, AL 36532
info@abbiglines.com

Interior Design & Formatting by:
Christine Borgford, Type A Formatting

All rights reserved. Published in the United States by Abbi Glines. This is a work of fiction. Names, characters, places and incidents either are the product of the author's imagination or are used fictitiously. Any resemblance to actual persons, living or dead, events, or locales, is entirely coincidental.

Sweet Little Lies

Chapter One

I'D DRIVEN FOR over an hour with nowhere to go. Tears were blurring my vision, my chest ached, and I wanted to curl up in a ball and sob freely. But there was no time for that. I had Heidi to think of. My sister. She was my first concern. Always my first concern. She could never know what had happened.

I no longer had a home or a job. I had this car I was driving. I had my sister. That was it. Heidi's care had been taken care of—or I thought it had been. Jasper had said he was going to pay ten years in advance but I wasn't sure he'd had a chance to do that yet. Even if he had how could I let him after what we'd learned? She was my sister. Mine. I should take care of her. Not him.

Just three hours ago my life had seemed perfect. I'd been happy and I was almost at the point where I could accept the security that came with Jasper Van Allan's love. I didn't blame him because he was an innocent bystander of the dark past too. Our circumstances weren't his fault or mine, but I should have known better than to trust love. It was a dangerous path that eventually uncovered lies that always led to ruin.

The home that Portia Van Allan had placed Heidi in for her long-term care loomed up ahead. I pulled over to take a breath before walking inside to face Heidi. She wouldn't understand why I was upset. I didn't want Heidi to know the ugliness of the world. Her heart was too big and her smile was too bright to ruin them with our reality. The lies that I now knew regarding her birth were secrets I'd keep. Heidi wouldn't understand them anyway. She loved our mother as I did. Our mother was a saint and I knew we'd never be the same without her.

The fact Heidi had been born to Portia Van Allan was a secret I would keep from her. Sharing who her birth mother was with Heidi was pointless, even if she could understand—I wasn't sure that was possible.

Heidi had been the most important person in my life for as long as I could remember. Even as a kid I knew Heidi's difference made her special. Precious. Easier to love.

As much as I hated Portia for tossing Heidi away because she'd been born with Down syndrome and that hadn't fit into her life, I was equally thankful she left her to my mother. Portia had given Heidi to us and she'd completed my family. It had always been the three of us. A perfect three that I would always cherish. Our mother had left us with beautiful memories. She had taught us that family was everything.

I pulled off the road and shifted the car into park. Crossing my arms over the steering wheel, I continued to cry. At this point, crying was all I could do. It's what I needed to do. I would cry and let it all out—my fear, my pain, my disbelief. Then I would dry my face, walk inside, and see my sister. When I walked inside, I planned to hug Heidi tightly and I would not fall apart in front of her. I was strong. My mother taught me to be strong. But right now, I needed Heidi. I missed her more than ever.

Beyond visiting Heidi, I had no idea what to do next. I had no idea where to turn.

Just as a loud sob escaped me, the passenger door of my car opened. My head jerked in the direction of the intruder and I was ready to scream when I realized it was Stone Richmond taking the seat beside me. His face was hard and cold like always.

Jasper's best friend hated me. I wasn't sure I liked him that much either. Stone was closed off and unfriendly. He didn't approve of Jasper and me. It was no secret Stone didn't think I was good enough for Jasper.

"Crying won't make it go away. Crying has never fucking fixed a damn thing," he said looking straight ahead out the window. His jaw clenched and his chiseled face appeared determined.

"I'm out of his life. What do you want?" I said as my voice cracked. Being taunted or corrected by Stone wasn't what I needed or wanted. Now or ever.

He turned his head to look at me. "I was expecting this," he said.

How could he have expected this? He didn't even know the details of what had transpired. I wanted to slap him and scream at him to release some of my pain. But I had never been violent.

"You want her to stay here, don't you? She likes it here," he nodded his head at the home Heidi lived in.

The facility was perfect for Heidi. She had friends. They gave her jobs that made her feel productive. She loved the activities. The home offered her a life that was safe but allowed her to be independent.

"It costs too much. Jasper wanted to pay ten years in advance. I don't know if he did, but I can't let him. Especially now," I replied unsure why he was asking about Heidi.

He reached over and took my keys out of the ignition. "You shouldn't be driving like this. You're too upset. It's dangerous."

I shot my arm out to snatch my car keys back from him. I was angry because his comments were unwelcome and out of line. "Give me my keys back. I'm fine."

He slipped them into his pocket. "No, Beulah. You aren't fine. You're a danger to not only yourself but others on the road. You need to calm down." He opened the passenger door. "I'll drive you up there. But you should wait until your face isn't red and splotchy from crying before you see your sister. I imagine that would upset her."

I agreed with him. I didn't want to agree with him. I didn't want him here. But for a moment, I wasn't alone. Even if it was Stone, he was helping calm me down. However, his sudden appearance still made no sense, unless Jasper had sent him.

"He sent you to find me, didn't he?" I asked him as I sat unmoving in the driver's seat.

Stone waited a moment, then climbed out of the car. He closed his car door, and walked around to open the driver's side door. I sat and watched him. Waiting for the confirmation that Jasper was trying to take care of me. My heart ached at the thought. Jasper couldn't do that. Not anymore.

As Stone stood waiting for me to get out of the car, I sighed and climbed out to face him. "Do you know? The lies? Did he tell you?"

Stone appeared unconcerned. His face showed no emotion. I wondered if it was his distaste for me that made him this way.

Because I'd seen him laugh, smile, and it had been startling. Stunning even. But he'd never done those things while looking at me.

"I've not seen or spoken to Jasper since earlier today in his office."

Frowning I wondered if he knew anything. Did he think we'd broken up? "Why . . . What are you doing here then? Were you looking for me?"

Stone lifted his chin and he looked slightly annoyed as he stared at something over my shoulder. "Understand something, Beulah. I've never disliked you. It was the lies I hated that would eventually come out. They had to. And when they did, I knew you'd be hurt. I knew you both would. I was trying to protect Jasper." He paused and moved his steely gaze back to me. "And I was trying to protect you."

What? I shook my head. That didn't make sense. "What lies did you know?" Because Jasper couldn't have known that Heidi was Portia's daughter. Or that Portia was my aunt. Were there more secrets I didn't know? I wasn't sure I could handle more, but I also knew I had to face the truth. Whatever it was.

"Jasper is a good man. He's got a good heart. But his life has been easy. It's been one with little destruction. He has never faced truly dark shit. I have. I see more than I want. I hear more than others want me to hear. When you arrived, I knew there was more to your sudden appearance. I knew there was more that you didn't understand. I did my own investigating. I found out the truth easily enough."

He knew and never said anything? He just let Jasper and me fall in love knowing our relationship was impossible? "You knew and didn't tell us? Why not tell Jasper? You want to protect him so badly, yet you let him . . . you let us go too far."

He let out a deep chuckle that exuded no warmth or real humor. "Beulah, he would never have believed me. The moment he laid eyes on you he was done. It was over. I saw it and I knew I couldn't stop what would happen."

I was ready to snap at him, but then I paused. Something didn't add up. I'd been so shocked and horrified by Heidi's name on that birth certificate that I hadn't thought it through. "Wait . . . Jasper is twenty-one year's old. Heidi is nineteen. We're the same age. That . . . Portia's story. It doesn't add up. Something is wrong." I looked at Stone for answers. He said he knew everything already. Did he know why Heidi was younger than Jasper?

Stone sighed. "What did she tell you?"

"That she was raped before she married Jasper's father, he married her even though she was pregnant. The baby had Down syndrome and she left her with my mother. But . . . Jasper. The timeline . . . something is wrong."

I was scared to hope that even the lies were wrong. But I found myself clinging to the possibility.

Chapter Two

STONE APPEARED TO be studying the woods behind me with a dark frown on his face. He didn't respond right away, and I let my imagination take over working out every scenario I could. I wanted to believe Heidi wasn't Portia's daughter.

"In the hospital records I found, Heidi was born to Portia Van Allan sixteen months after Jasper's birth." He looked at me then. "There are photos in the attic of the Van Allan house that I looked through while staying there the past month. The photos are of Portia pregnant in a white gown, and Jasper is a toddler beside her."

"What? But . . . she wasn't raped? Why did she say she was?" Nothing made sense. The lies continued to unravel, and there were lies on top of more lies. What could I believe?

"Heidi is a Van Allan. Half of the Van Allan inheritance should be hers. She has a right to something. If anyone knew the truth, that the Van Allans had a child and gave her away, there could be lawsuits filed on Heidi's behalf . . . by you."

I didn't understand. None of this made sense and nothing was clicking into place. You couldn't just give a kid away. There were photos of her pregnant with Jasper beside her. People had to know she had another baby. "She couldn't have just had a baby and everyone forgot it existed."

He gave a short nod of agreement. "That's what I thought too. Then," he stopped and took a long deep breath. I could tell by his posture and the look on his face that I didn't want to hear this. He didn't want to tell me either. "There was a small closed casket funeral for Heidi Clarisse Van Allan who died at birth."

What? What! I shook my head in disbelief. "No," was all I could say. My throat was thick. My chest felt as if a ton of bricks had been dumped on it. How could two humans be so cold and cruel? To claim their child was dead and get rid of it because it's not what they wanted. My beautiful sweet sister was the most special person on earth. I felt hate deep inside of me start to burn. It wasn't an emotion I was familiar with, but it was there and building.

"With the Van Allan money, they were allowed to pay off anyone to keep the truth about Heidi a secret. They never spoke of her again. The people in their world are so consumed with themselves they don't care about others. The death of a baby—they sent their condolences, and in time everything was forgotten." The look on Stone's face was pure disgust as he described how this could go away so easily.

"They just gave her away. They dropped money and a child on my mother. Then not another word. There was nothing from them. Heidi is the most perfect human I know. But they didn't care." I said the words aloud trying to comprehend it. I never would though. They were both monsters. Terrible, horrible people with dark souls. I was thankful Heidi never knew them. That she had my mother to love her. My mother was the best.

"Portia already relies solely on Jasper to keep up her life. She wouldn't let it go so far that you and Jasper went any further being related. But she had to tell a story that made her appear less horrible if that is possible. The rape was her way of adding an excuse and attempting to get sympathy or at least understanding. She doesn't want him to know the truth. But in her haste, she didn't tie up all her loose ends to her lie. Jasper is going to realize the same thing you did. He'll demand the truth. He won't be able to forgive her."

How could anyone? How did a mother do that? "How do I face Heidi without breaking apart? I won't be able to hold her and not weep."

His gaze shifted up the hill toward the beautiful home that was Heidi's safe place. "You're strong. I've watched you. You can do this. Do what you always do when you visit her. Play some kickball. Let her do whatever she wants to do today. Enjoy her. When you're ready to leave, your car will be waiting for you. I'll drive you to the house and park it, then I can walk back here to pick up my Rover."

"I just leave her here? I don't know if Jasper paid them already. If he didn't, I need to figure out my next move. If he did then . . . then I don't know . . . I don't know what to do anymore."

Stone shifted his eyes back to me. "Heidi is a Van Allan. A Van Allan that lived in poverty in a trailer park while her parents traveled the world and lived in luxury. That money is as much hers as Jaspers."

His words sunk in. Slowly. I'd seen the birth certificate, and I knew it was real. But I finally let my mind go there, truly accepting that Jasper was Heidi's sister by blood. She wasn't mine. The girl that I loved more than myself wasn't my real sister.

"She will always be your sister," he added as if he had read my thoughts. "Your connection can't be broken by something as simple as who gave you life. The bond you have with her is stronger than any blood."

He was right. Heidi and I were connected. That would never be taken from me. "I can't see him or talk to him," I whispered. "Not yet. Maybe not for a while. He's going to think this through and realize the story we were told was impossible. But I can't."

"It's best you don't. I can handle things. For now, get in the car and let me take you to visit your sister. It will put your mind at rest to see she is taken care of."

I did as I was told. After walking around the car, I climbed into the passenger side. It was funny how easy it was to obey Stone. The authority in his voice should annoy me, anger me even, but I found solace in his assertive words. His commanding presence was calming, and I needed that desperately.

Stone drove us in silence back onto the road. From there, it was a short distance up the hill to the facility. The home that had been a godsend for Heidi after losing our mom. Heidi had adored our mother. She'd always felt equal because Momma made sure she did. If I did something, she made sure Heidi did it too. Even if it took a lot of help from both us.

After Stone parked the car, I sat there staring straight ahead. "I never want Heidi to know the truth. Our mother, she was *our* mother. Heidi loves her and misses her. Momma was Heidi's world. This isn't something Heidi will understand."

I don't know why I was telling Stone. It wasn't as if he was going to walk inside and tell Heidi the terrible truth. But I needed to tell someone, and right now he was all I had.

"She doesn't need to know. She has you. That's all she needs."

I agreed with all of my heart. "What if . . . what if Portia wants to see her? Talk to her? If Jasper throws her out . . . What if Portia tried to use Heidi to get Van Allan money?"

That woman wasn't someone I wanted near my sister. She was evil and cruel, and had no heart. She was selfish and cold. Heidi was nothing like her.

"She won't," he said. "There's too much at stake. More than her being broke and penniless. What she did wasn't just cruel, it was illegal."

"Are you sure?"

"Positive. I've verified her actions were and still are illegal," he said with confidence.

I turned my head and looked at him. "But she may decide to face her lies."

Stone leaned closer to me—closer than he'd ever been. His gaze was intense and invited no argument. Where Jasper was kind and warm, Stone wasn't. "The first thing you're going to have to learn is to trust me, Beulah. Because I don't lie, and I swear to you that Portia won't come near Heidi."

He didn't add that he wouldn't let her. But his expression was so determined that I didn't question it. It was hard not to believe his sincerity.

"Okay," I whispered.

He nodded his head toward the door. "Go. Visit with Heidi. Forget the shit from today. I'm going to text an address to you. Drive your car there after your visit."

That last part threw me off. "Why?" I asked.

His left eyebrow lifted slightly. "Do you have a place to stay tonight?"

Oh. I hadn't thought of that. I shook my head.

"Didn't think so. I'll text you an address. When you leave, head there."

I opened my mouth to ask him more, but he climbed out of the car and walked away. He left just like that. Stone had shown up out of the blue with answers, not lies. He'd reassured me Heidi was okay. He hadn't let me fall apart. I had felt stronger with him there.

If I was honest, I didn't want him to leave. During our brief talk in my car, he'd made me feel secure. When he spoke, I believed his words. He spoke with certainty that you simply couldn't question.

My phone dinged, and I pulled it from my back pocket. There was an address just like he had said. I had a place to sleep tonight and time to figure out what we would do next. What would I do?

I removed the keys from the ignition and got out of the car from where I sat in the passenger side seat. I knew visiting Heidi would help me. Seeing her smile and knowing she was okay was what I needed right now. The last name on her birth certificate meant nothing. Heidi was an Edwards. She always would be.

The Van Allans had buried her years ago. Their name went with that time and place. The cruelty of their actions was heartbreaking. I couldn't help but be grateful she'd been given a better life. I knew we loved Heidi the way she deserved.

"Beulah, we weren't expecting you!" I forced a smile as Tammy, one of Heidi's favorite nurses, greeted me with surprise. "Heidi and May are crafting in the activity room right now. They are going to be so excited to see you. Even if you don't have any cookies or cupcakes."

I rarely visited Heidi empty-handed, but then I also always came when she was expecting me. "Hopefully the surprise of seeing me outweighs not having treats," I replied.

"Oh, it will!"

I headed back to the activity room. Heidi had learned to crochet and she loved it. She was making pot holders and dish rags the last time I came to see her. I wondered if that was what they were up to today.

Just as I was about to reach the crafting room, the door to the office opened and Mrs. Shell, the accounts manager, walked out. I always made payments for Heidi's care here to her.

"Beulah, I just got your payment for Heidi. It came through the computer system. That's wonderful that the Van Allans have decided to pay upfront for the next ten years. I know that takes the monthly concern off your shoulders. You can focus on getting that degree you were talking about instead of always working." She winked and walked on down the hallway without waiting on my response.

Heidi's home was paid for now. I wouldn't have to worry. But knowing it was paid with Van Allan money bothered me.

Chapter Three

THE BRICK PAVED path led to a three-story apartment building that appeared to have been recently restored. Each floor looked like it held only one apartment. The plaque on the outside of the building said it was built in 1920. Stone had been living at Jasper's, so I wasn't sure whose apartment this was.

There were three cars parked outside. A black Hummer, a white Range Rover, and a red Porsche. Stone's Black Range Rover wasn't present.

I checked the address again. He hadn't given me an apartment number or a name. Maybe I was at the wrong place. I had enough money to find an inexpensive hotel room for the night. My other option was knocking on the apartment doors to ask the occupants if they were expecting me, which seemed a bit creepy.

Before I could think it through much longer, a girl with long almost black hair emerged from the front door of the building. She was all legs and incredibly thin. She looked like a runway model. Her shorts were tiny and showed off her legs—they were longer than most people's bodies. A pair of aviator sunglasses were perched on her head although the sun had already begun to set.

Her gaze swung to me as she started walking in my direction. I watched until she was almost beside my car before I opened my door to see if she was coming to talk to me. Either she was expecting me, or she was walking over to ask me what I was doing parked at this elite apartment complex. A complex that didn't seem to have any traffic and no parked cars out front that cost less than one hundred grand.

Stepping out of the car, I had to tilt my head back to look at her. With the heels she was wearing she was at least six-foot-three. She swung her hair over her shoulder and gave me a tight smile. "I was going to ask if you were Beulah, but now that I see you I know the answer to that question. Figures," she rolled her eyes and turned to walk back to the building.

I didn't move. I wasn't sure what she meant exactly. She glanced back over her shoulder. "Are you coming or not?" she asked exasperatedly.

She didn't seem very happy about this. I wasn't sure I wanted to intrude on someone who didn't want me there. "Uh, I don't think so," I replied making up my mind before she could snap at me again.

That stopped her from sauntering away with her heels and long legs. She spun around again looking very much like someone walking the catwalk. Her left hand landed on her hip—or the bone that was covered with skin—and glared at me. "Seriously? Stone went to all this trouble, and you're just going to leave?"

What trouble had he gone through? I hadn't meant for him to have any trouble. I started to ask when his Rover pulled into the exclusive parking lot. I had never been relieved to see Stone. The feeling was new but I was definitely glad he was here.

He got out and walked over to me shooting a glance toward the girl. "You coming inside?" he asked shifting his gaze back to me.

I looked nervously at the unknown female who was no longer scowling but was smiling politely. "She is a little apprehensive. Can't convince her to come inside," the girl's tone was sweet and sounded as if she were talking about a small child.

"You've got nowhere else to go, Beulah." His demeanor turned frustrated just that quickly.

I wasn't being stubborn. He hadn't been here, and it was obvious the girl didn't want me here. I decided against saying that though since this was her apartment. Or at least I assumed it was her apartment.

"I know," I replied. Then it hit me. I had nothing. All my things were at Jasper's. I'd been so upset over everything else and trying to focus on Heidi while my mind was turning over all the horrors I'd been told today. "I don't," I said glancing back inside my car for anything I might have left in there. "have my things," I finished.

"They're inside. I picked them up earlier," Stone replied as if this made perfect sense.

"You did?" I asked confused.

"How else were you going to get them?" He didn't expect an answer to that question. I couldn't help answering him anyway.

"I don't know."

"This is my building. I rent out the other two apartments. Presley lives in mine," he said as he began to walk toward the building. He expected me to follow him. I closed my car door and looked at the building more closely. Did he own the entire building? I didn't think he worked, much less that he would own a building. He was always partying and sleeping in Stone's pool house.

The girl was walking with more of a swing in her hips now. I was assuming she was Presley. He acted as if I knew who that was. She hadn't told me her name.

"You're taking me to Manhattan soon though. I want to see your new flat there. I'd rather live there with you than here in Savannah," she said in a flirty voice as she gazed back at him.

"The top floor is mine. The rooftop is shared. Chantel and Fiona are on the second floor. And Marty and Mack—they're on the first floor."

He had ignored her comment. Although I was listening to him tell me about the building it was hard to miss her body had suddenly tensed. She didn't like being ignored and I doubted men ignored her often. I was confounded because she was living in his apartment, so what did that make them? I'd seen Stone with a lot of women. Jasper had mentioned Stone getting a ring for a Margot once, but that was it. He hadn't seemed happy about the idea.

Having a woman live in his apartment that he never stayed at seemed more Stone-like than his sudden hero act. He'd been a jerk since the day I'd met him. But today he'd been there when I thought I had no one. I was confused with my feelings for him.

"Chantel is in the Caribbean with Dameon. Luke broke up with him last night and he was having a meltdown, so she took him to the islands to get away. Luke is doing my shoot tomorrow. I'm sure I'll get to hear his side of the story. He's such a slut though. We all warned Dameon when he started dating him."

Presley was telling this story so dramatically I felt like she was explaining the missed episode of a television show. Stone didn't seem very interested in any of it. He stepped in front of Presley and opened the door. "I wanted to add a keypad for the lock so we wouldn't need keys to the building but there are rules in the city with any structure considered to be historical. When I bought it to restore, I had to keep several things within the time period it was built. There are specific things you can't touch to be considered a historical structure—the door for instance. It had to be restored and the original could not be replaced." He waved his hand for us to come inside.

Presley went ahead of me quickly and leaned in to kiss Stone lingeringly on the lips. "I missed you," she whispered.

He didn't look pleased with the affection but he didn't turn her away either. I noticed his hand even rested on her waist for a moment.

"There is no elevator. Again, had to stick with historical restoration code," he said as I walked inside.

"Which is a pain when you have bags to carry upstairs," Presley whined.

I'd been so silent I decided I should say something. "I bet carrying the groceries up can be difficult." I figured that sounded like something she would be annoyed with. This place was beautiful and I couldn't imagine she had any reason to complain. Telling her that wouldn't win her over though.

She laughed. "Why would I carry groceries up the stairs? The delivery service does that when we order."

There was a delivery service for groceries? I started to ask that out loud and decided against it. She'd just find that amusing too.

Stone started up the stairs, and Presley rushed to stay beside him. I followed them up as she whispered and giggled in his ear. He never responded, but he never pushed her away either.

I didn't belong here. I suddenly realized that I didn't belong anywhere and I hadn't since my mother passed away. I was determined not to feel sorry for myself. I had a bed to sleep in tonight. My situation could be worse.

Chapter Four

STONE HAD SAID the building was historical. I hadn't realized that meant the apartment would look like something from the Great Gatsby era. It was as if I'd walked into the book itself. The outside had been stunning and true to that time period. It was surprising because I'd imagined something more modern inside, and considerably less stunning.

"This is," I said turning in circles taking in the entrance of his apartment, "amazing." Even the furnishings, although most were newer and few were real antiques, fit the architectural style.

"You like it?" There was pride in his tone.

"Who wouldn't?" I asked still looking at all the detail.

"You won't be so thrilled about everything when you realize the bathrooms have those old claw-foot tubs instead of a nice big Jacuzzi," Presley said with a sigh as if this was a real burden for her.

Stone didn't respond. I wondered if she paid him rent. If living in this gorgeous apartment was free for her, it was incredibly rude of her to complain. I thought claw-foot tubs sounded cool.

"When did you do this? I thought you'd been at college in New Hampshire until this summer." I knew I'd heard Jasper talk about living in New Hampshire with roommates.

"I like restoring old things. It's a hobby. I started two years ago and finished it up this past fall. Most of the big items were completed by contractors with lots of phone calls. It was hard to travel here to check on things. Coming here instead of staying in Manhattan was nice though."

Presley sighed dramatically. She did that a lot. "I love Manhattan. I hate your mother, but I love the city."

Again, Stone ignored her.

"Your room will be the third door on the left," Stone said. "There is a bathroom connected to it, and if you can suffer through the antiquated features it's yours to use," he said the last bit with obvious disdain. Presley's earlier comment was not well received.

"Thank you, Stone. I appreciate this. Really, I do. And I'll spend tomorrow finding a place to live. I won't be a hindrance."

He frowned. "You've got a lot to figure out. The room isn't being used. It's yours. Use it. Don't worry about a place to live right now. Deal with the other shit first."

I didn't look at Presley to see her response. She wouldn't be as agreeable as him. I'd already figured out she wasn't crazy about me being here.

"Clover is coming to visit soon. She'll need somewhere to sleep," Presley said quickly. "That's my sister," she added as she shot a glare my way.

"Clover can sleep in your king-size bed with you," Stone told her. The authority in his voice was subtle but unmistakable. 'That room is Beulah's."

Presley inhaled sharply. "Are you fucking her? Is that it? Jasper tossed her out because he caught you with her, didn't he? I can't believe you'd do this to me! You've never thrown one in my face. All your sluts, even Margot—"

"That will be all, Presley!"

I jumped, startled by his loud command. Presley immediately broke into tears. "You always hurt me. Always. Your mother doesn't think I'm good enough. That's it, isn't it!" she wailed.

"Not the fucking drama. Jesus, save it for your friends. I'm not in the mood for it." Stone's voice was still louder than normal and angry. Like a parent talking to a child. "Go wail to Fiona. Drink vodka or some shit. But not in here."

Presley pointed at me. "And leave you alone with her? To fuck in my house? Your mother would hate her too! She wants you to marry Margot!" The shrill of her voice made me wince as did her accusations.

"I am not fucking Beulah. However, this is my home. If I want to fuck someone here, I will. My mother has never and will never have a say in who I do or don't fuck. I don't owe you anything, Presley. You owe me a lot. Remember that and go cool off. Preferably not in this apartment." Stone turned to me. "I'm going to have some whiskey now. Presley often drives me to drink in short amounts of time. Can I get you anything, or would you rather go hide out in the sanctuary of your room?"

'That! You say things like that, and it's mean. Cruel, Stone! Cruel! You act like I mean nothing to you. Just like your father—"

"For the love of God, would you take that yammering and find a friend to punish with it!" He was loud again. Almost shouting.

Presley spun around on her heel and ran out the door in tears. After she slammed the door behind her, he sighed and shook his head as he walked to the bar and took a glass down from the rack beside it.

"Want a drink?" he asked again.

"No, thank you. I think I'll just go to the room."

"Don't blame you."

I stood there watching him trying to figure out why he was in a relationship with a woman he didn't seem to care for particularly. He also wasn't faithful to her and she was aware of that. It wasn't my business. He'd been nothing but generous to me today. But the hard, cruel man he was flickered there in his eyes while Presley, as annoying and spoiled as she was, had cried.

"Is she okay? Your girlfriend?" I didn't want to cause a problem with them. He should have reassured her there was nothing going on with us.

He glanced back at me then took a drink of his whiskey. "Presley?"

Of course, Presley. Who else would I be talking about? I didn't say that though, I simply nodded.

"She'll be fine. She's dramatic. It's her nature and always has been. You'll get used to it."

I would get used to her screaming and crying? I doubted it. "She does this a lot?"

He smirked and took a drink. "There are several reasons I was sleeping in Jasper's pool house. What you witnessed was one of those reasons."

"Then . . . why do you stay together?" I was pushing it. I needed to shut up. This was not my home and he was letting me stay here.

"That's a story too convoluted to get into. I've not had enough to drink to unload that one. Maybe another time."

I deserved a more curt response from him for my nosiness, but he'd been kinder in his response.

"I'm sorry. I shouldn't have asked."

He didn't agree or disagree. Instead, he continued to drink and stare at me with his bored expression. He wanted me to go. After that debacle, I imagined he needed peace and quiet, not me asking a million questions.

"Good night and thank you again," I said before turning to walk down the hallway toward the room he said was mine.

"You'll find your things in the closet," he called out.

"Okay, thank you," I replied. I'd said thank you a lot. But I didn't know how else to express my gratitude. If this was a regular bachelor pad I'd offer to clean it. It wasn't though, the place was immaculate. I'd have to find a way to pay him back for all he'd done for me today.

"And Beulah, Presley is my stepsister."

Chapter Five

I UNDERSTOOD STEPSIBLINGS weren't related by blood, but pondering Presley and Stone together was still disturbing. Did they grown up together in the same house? Because if that was true, their relationship was . . . well . . . gross. Wasn't it? I couldn't decide if I was being judgmental or not. Maybe I should be more open-minded. They were obviously in a relationship of some kind. Her angry outburst when she assumed he was sleeping with me led me to believe she was his girlfriend.

If Stone was trying to give me a distraction from my thinking about Jasper being my cousin, and my sister not being my sister but Jasper's sister, then he had just accomplished it. But only for a moment.

I laid my head back and closed my eyes as I soaked in the large claw-foot tub.

This morning I had woken up in a dream. It was a fantasy that dissolved abruptly when I realized I loved a man I shouldn't love. I'd had sex with Jasper, my cousin. I guess when I looked at it that way, what I had done was so much worse than Stone and his stepsister. Jasper and my mother were sisters. My stomach turned at the thought.

Just as quickly as I'd been handed happiness, it had been snatched away. And there was Heidi to think about. She'd never know the truth. Even if she did, I wasn't sure she'd understand. My mother was our mother. I didn't care who gave birth to my sister. Portia Van Allan may have brought her into this world, but it was my mother who loved her, protected her, taught her, and raised her. Heidi missed Momma, but it didn't weigh on her every day like it did me. She found happiness in life so easily. I had always envied her that. Being around her made me happy. Even if it was for a short time.

I wouldn't fight Jasper if he wanted to pay for Heidi's care. I knew it was his way of helping. After all we'd learned, she was his sister too. Their biological relationship would change things. I couldn't expect it not to.

Then there was my heart—would it always ache when I thought of Jasper? Could I one day see him and not hope for the impossible?

The ringing of my phone interrupted my thoughts and I sat up to see where I had left it. When it rang again, I turned my head toward the sound to find I'd put it on the vanity. I didn't want to get out of the tub yet, but it could be Heidi calling. That was the only reason I hadn't turned my phone off.

Jasper didn't come find me today. He didn't come looking for me. I'd left him at his house begging me to forget the truth. When he didn't even understand the truth himself. I couldn't forget. My heart may wish I could but my head wouldn't allow it.

Standing, I grabbed the towel that was on the white and gold stand beside the tub and wrapped it around me. It was even more lush than the towels at the Van Allans. Hurrying over to the vanity I reached for my phone only to see Jasper's name on the screen. I jerked my hand back as if it were a snake. I couldn't talk to him. He had thought through Portia's lie by now and realized things didn't added up. I wouldn't be the one to tell him the truth though. Hearing his voice . . . I wasn't ready. Stone would have to tell Jasper and show him what he'd found.

We had nothing more to say. Did we? What could we say? Sorry we committed incest? I cringed even admitting that word to myself. I didn't like to think of it that way. I still couldn't believe it was true. Falling in love with Jasper would have been the best memory I'd ever made, but now it had become the most twisted.

Fate didn't like me much. I was beginning to accept that it intended to beat me up continually.

I stepped away from the phone as the ringing ended. He'd get my voicemail. I prayed he didn't leave a message because I couldn't listen to it. I was convinced that would only make our current situation worse.

I waited to see if the voicemail alert would ding. I knew hiding from my phone wasn't possible. Turning it off and trying to disappear wasn't possible. I had to find a way to accept this. I needed strength to not fall apart at the sound of his voice.

Moments passed and no email alert. Nothing. I sighed, relieved that I wouldn't be taunted by a voicemail I couldn't listen to. The sound of a slamming door echoed down the hall and I jumped. Holding my towel tighter around me, I walked back into the bedroom expecting to hear Presley crying and screaming. But it wasn't Presley's voice I heard. It was Jasper's.

My eyes flew to the door to make sure I'd locked it. What was he doing here?

The thick, huge doors muffled their voices, but Jasper was loud. He was shouting. I couldn't understand exactly what he was saying but I heard my name. With each pause of his shouting I strained to hear Stone. He wasn't speaking loud enough if he was even responding to Jasper at all.

Footsteps started down the hall and right before they got to my door, I heard Stone's voice say, "Don't." The command was clear but the door handle for my room began to wiggle.

"Beulah! Talk to me. Please, I can't . . ." he paused. "I can't lose you completely. What Stone found out about my parents . . . I'm sorry. It's so fucking twisted. Don't hate me because of my last name. Talk to me. There's got to be more to this. We need each other."

I backed away. I wasn't ready. It's possible I might never be ready. Tears burned my eyes and I blinked, forcing them to fall freely. No one was here to see me break apart.

"She needs time," Stone told him.

"Beulah. Listen, I don't even know what to believe. The one thing I'm sure of is I love you. Don't shut me out. We need each other."

I sank down on the edge of the bed and held onto my towel tightly. Hearing the pain in his voice was crushing. I didn't want to hurt him. But the truth had hurt us both.

"For once, stop being so goddamn selfish." Stone was angry. I didn't want him to fight with Jasper because of me. This wasn't his problem. I wasn't his to protect.

"Beulah—"

"LEAVE!" Stone shouted, stopping Jasper from saying more.

There was silence.

Finally, I heard Jasper speaking to Stone. "Why are you doing this? Why are you keeping her from me? You saw me happy and you hated it!"

At first there was a pause. I didn't think Stone was going to respond. I prepared myself for Jasper to say more to me. Glancing toward the bathroom from my perch on the bed, I decided to walk back inside and close that door. It helped to muffle their voices and gave me some privacy to pull myself together.

"Beulah's been through enough. She's not like you. Her world is vastly different. Give her time to work through this. She needs to find her ground without this added drama."

I froze listening to Stone's words. They weren't flattering but they were factual.

"She's not like us. Isn't that what you mean? Because you're from the same world I am. Look around you." Jasper wasn't yelling anymore but his anger was still obvious.

"No. My world has always been different from yours. Don't kid yourself. Now, leave. I've had enough bullshit for one night. I need a fucking break."

I waited to see if Jasper would walk away. I wondered if he'd do as Stone asked of him, or if they'd continue to fight. I'd get dressed and walk out there to stop them if they did. I couldn't let them ruin their friendship because of me. It wasn't fair to either of them.

"When you're ready to talk, call me. I'll always be here," Jasper said with his voice raised for me to hear inside the bathroom, but his tone didn't sound as harsh.

I bit my bottom lip to muffle a sob as tears began to roll down my face again. Their retreating footsteps meant this interlude was over. He was leaving. I listened for more shouting but I heard nothing. After several moments, I went to the closet and found my clothing hung up instead of in my travel bag. They looked lost inside the massive closet complete with a full-length mirror and chandelier.

Tomorrow I had to leave. Stone was right. This wasn't my world. I needed to stop living in it. So far it had only brought me sorrow.

Chapter Six

THE APARTMENT WAS quiet. I never heard Presley return last night and I had fallen asleep the moment I got into bed. I had taken my time getting dressed and packing up my things. I'd hoped to hear someone moving about in the apartment this morning, but it was after eight and no doors had opened or closed. There was no sound at all. It was silent.

I opened the bedroom door slowly and glanced down the hallway. The lights were off. The sunlight from the large windows throughout the apartment provided enough light to see where I was going.

I felt weird leaving without saying anything to Stone.

At the end of the hallway the smell of coffee met my nose. I figured I would encounter either Stone or Presley. If it was Presley, maybe she'd be nicer when she saw me carrying my duffle bag. My leaving should put her in a good mood.

I turned, walking in the direction of where I smelled coffee and found the kitchen. Stone's back was to me as he stood watching the news on a large flat screen television on the wall opposite the doorway. He was wearing a dress shirt, tie and jeans. He held a cup of coffee in his hand and frowned as the news reported about some Senator liking a porn website on Facebook that had gone viral.

His shoulders were broad, but his size seemed pronounced in the fitted oxford dress shirt. The guy at the pool who laughed and drank with friends wasn't the same man in front of me. This man held secrets. He was important—or he appeared to be. I'd thought he was an elitist snob and spoiled. After yesterday, I wasn't so sure about either of those things. He wasn't homeless. I was wrong about that for sure.

I thought about the pool party and wondered why Presley hadn't been there. Did he keep her separate from his friends? Why did she live here? Their story wasn't my business but I was curious. Stone had gotten under my skin since the moment I met him. He was helping me and had even stood up to Jasper to keep him away from me—that had changed my perception of him. His actions over the past twenty-four hours made me want to know more about him.

"There's coffee and some pastries from the bakery in town. You're welcome to both, or you can continue to stand there and check me out while my back is turned."

He turned his head just enough for me to see his smirk, then he pointed with the hand holding his cup toward the coffee and pastries he'd just mentioned. "Help yourself. There's some of everything."

I was embarrassed to have been caught staring at him but I was about to leave. I doubted I'd see him again any time soon, if ever. That thought shouldn't bother me. But it did.

His eyes dropped to the duffle bag in my left hand. "You're not leaving, Beulah. You have nowhere to go."

"My presence here is causing problems. Presley, then Jasper—" I began but was interrupted.

"Presley will be over it today. Jasper was expected. I expect more from him. He has been spoiled the majority of his life and that leads one to believe they can have whatever they want. When they're told no, they react without thought. Now, have some breakfast, and afterward put your things away. Then I have somewhere to take you."

He spoke as if his orders were law. My opinion was of no consequence. I didn't like being controlled or handled, but on the other hand, I wasn't ready to say no. Walking away from the only security I had at the moment seemed foolish. I battled with what to do mentally as he went back to watching the news.

I opened my mouth twice to say something. No argument or quirky response came. Finally, I sat my duffle bag down and put my purse on top of it. I gave in and walked over to fix myself a cup of coffee from a very ordinary coffee pot. I didn't expect that of Stone. Especially not coming from his world of wealth. The Van Allans had several fancy machines that produced coffee, espresso, cappuccinos, and then that French press I hated to use.

"This is a regular coffee pot," I said glancing back at Stone.

He didn't look at me when he spoke. "Coffee is meant to be simple."

I couldn't argue with that. "Did you go to the bakery this morning?" I asked wondering when he could have gone. I had listened for the door. If he was quiet when he left, I knew the thick walls in the apartment would have muffled the sound though.

"Presley has the bakery make daily deliveries," he replied still watching the television.

That seemed odd. I wouldn't have thought Presley ate pastries. She was so thin. Eating this every morning would put weight on anyone. I picked one that looked like a croissant with chocolate glaze. I wasn't positive it was a croissant, but it looked delicious. I didn't eat lunch or dinner yesterday and I was starving. I wondered if he'd mind if I ate two. Or more importantly, if Presley would mind.

Once the news went to a commercial, he turned to watch me as I stood at the bar with my breakfast. "You can have a seat at the table if you'd like. And eat more than one of those. There are too many."

I reached over to pick up the strawberry muffin, placed it on my plate, and then headed for the table. "Thank you. I woke up hungry," I admitted.

He took a sip of his coffee and studied me. I found myself hoping the news would come back on so I could eat without his laser focus on me. Stone made me nervous because you couldn't tell what he was thinking. His expressions were always serious. He always seemed closed off, brooking no discussion.

"How are you with elderly people?"

That was the oddest and most random question I'd ever been asked.

"What do you mean exactly?"

The news returned after the commercial and he turned it off by touching something on his phone. I'd never seen that before.

"You handled Portia and she's a high maintenance bitch. You're patient, hard-working, and trustworthy. I would assume you'd be good with an elderly slightly senile lady."

When I didn't say anything right away he continued.

"Geraldine Mayweather is a friend of mine. She's at the point in life where she needs help with her daily activities. Cleaning, cooking small meals, reminding her to take pills, and at times where the bathroom is or what year it is are a few things she could use assistance with. I think you'd be a perfect fit to work with someone in her situation."

Oh. A job. One that I knew I could do. Stone said it just like that.

"That sounds great," I replied quickly. "Thank you. I don't know how I can repay you for all you've done."

"Don't thank me yet. I'm going to introduce you to Geraldine. She'll have to approve of you of course. It's her decision."

I nodded. "Of course. When can we go?"

"As soon as you're finished eating and put your bag back in the closet in your bedroom."

"Thank you," I repeated.

He sat his cup in the sink and left the room without another word.

I finished the chocolate croissant and strawberry muffin then rinsed my dish and both cups. After I dried the dishes, I located the correct cabinets so that I could put them away.

As I was walking to pick up my duffle bag, the front door opened. I froze hoping it was Stone opening the door.

Heels clicked on the marble floor and were headed toward the kitchen. There was no way I was going to escape her. Bracing myself, I picked up my duffle and faced the door just as Presley entered the kitchen.

She was in the same clothes she'd worn last night. Her face had been washed clean of makeup, and her eyes appeared slightly bloodshot. She strutted past me. "Leaving already?" she asked in a bored tone.

I didn't want to answer her but I couldn't just walk out of the room without acknowledging her. That would be rude. "No, not leaving yet. I was, but I'm not now. I will be soon." I added the last to hopefully avoid a screaming fit.

"Why are there pastries here? Jesus, who eats these calories in the morning?" she turned and looked at me with horror. "Your hips will only get bigger eating like this."

She didn't eat the pastries. Which meant she didn't order them.

"I didn't, I mean those aren't—" I wasn't sure how to respond to her.

She rolled her eyes. "Well, they aren't Stones. He only eats egg whites and whole wheat toast for breakfast. I make it for him."

The fact she'd talked to me as if I were a child caught in a lie wasn't what left me speechless. It was that the only explanation had to be . . . Stone ordered the pastries.

For me.

Chapter Seven

HE DIDN'T WANT me to know he'd bought me pastries, so I didn't tell him about my conversation with Presley. I'd gone back to the bedroom, unpacked my bag, and then waited at the door for him. He came out of the kitchen wearing an annoyed expression.

"We'll take both cars in case Geraldine decides you're a good fit and hires you. You'll need your car to get back here this evening."

My keys were already in my purse, so I nodded and followed him out the door. Before he could lock the door behind us, the sound of heels clicking echoed through the front foyer as Presley ran toward him.

"Have a good day, baby!" she said as she threw herself into his chest.

The stepsister thing was all I could see. It was disturbing, but I forced myself not to think about it. I didn't know the whole story.

He didn't return her hug, and that made her more desperate. She began kissing his face.

He took both her arms in his hands and set her back from him. "Presley, please."

She stuck out her bottom lip in a pout. "When will you be back?"

"When I'm done with my day. Goodbye." And with that, he left.

I didn't look at her as I followed behind him. That had been awkward. And a little sad. Stone wasn't cruel to Presley. He also didn't give her the affection she wanted or expected, which I gathered at some point he must have.

We walked silently down the stairs and out the doors to the parking lot. Only one other car was parked there—the red Porsche. It looked like something Presley would drive.

"Follow me," he said. His voice was commanding and invited no nonsense.

I stumbled behind him as he walked to his vehicle.

It wasn't until I was in my car driving that the previous day's events began to replay in my head. The heaviness in my stomach and the ache in my chest that hadn't gone away were constant reminders. I thought of my mother and how she must have felt when Portia came to her with Heidi. I knew my mother would never have turned her away even without the money. But how exhausted and scared she had to have been at times. With two little girls, no help, and one who needed the extra care that Heidi required. The money they'd given her had only lasted for a short time. Heidi's medical bills added up fast in the beginning.

Heidi didn't walk until she was five. We were in the kitchen coloring at the table when she took her first steps. I'd had to keep reminding her not to eat her crayons while Momma made biscuits for dinner. She made biscuits whenever money was tight.

I had dropped a green crayon and I had stood to pick it up when Heidi tottered to her feet and took her first steps toward the fallen crayon. She'd said proudly, "I get it."

Mom had made cupcakes to celebrate after we ate the biscuits with sausage gravy. The image of her hugging Heidi tightly and telling her how proud she was still stuck in my head. But now . . . Now that I knew Heidi wasn't her daughter, it made my mother even more special. And I hadn't thought that was possible.

I remembered when Mom would kiss my head at bedtime—she'd tell me to get in bed and that she'd be in shortly. I'd fall asleep before she could get there because Heidi wouldn't rest until Mom had rocked her. It took hours some nights. Otherwise, Heidi would cry. The dark scared her, even with me in the same room. Mom would bend down and whisper in my ear, "I couldn't live this life without you my Beulah beauty. You're my source of strength. Heidi is my joy, but you sweet girl, are my heart. Never forget how dearly I love you. Even when I can't always hold you as long as you want or tuck you in at night."

Those words made more sense now. I understood what she never told me. It was something I didn't need to know. I missed Mom every day. She always told me I was her strength, but she was mine. I didn't know how I could be hers.

My attention snapped back to the road when Stone switched on his blinker and turned into a driveway in front of me. There was a massive stone wall with a wrought iron gate with the letter M in the center of it. Stone leaned out his window and said something to a small black box and the gate opened slowly. I followed him inside the fortress, or whatever this was. Magnolia trees lined the driveway until it opened up and a small castle appeared. My jaw dropped at the sight of all the grandeur. I'd never seen a house like this one. It looked like a bonafide castle.

Stone pulled around to park right in front of the steps leading up to the impressive doors. There were even stone lions at the bottom of the stairs. I parked behind him and sat there taking it in. Did someone actually build this to look like a castle? And why?

Stone was standing in front of me blocking my view and I shifted my eyes to meet his. He shrugged as if this was to be expected. After turning my car off, I grabbed my keys and got out of the car.

"What in the world?" I asked. My words were laden with awe.

"She's a bit eccentric. Her husband indulged her whimsies when he was alive. This house was one of them."

"Uh, this is more than whimsy," I said walking to meet him on the stairs.

"Not to Victor Mayweather."

I started to ask more when one of the doors opened and a tiny lady with snow-white hair pulled up in piggy tails appeared. "Stone! I thought the milkman was here. He's late," she said throwing her hands up in the air.

"The milkman won't be coming today Gerry love. He retired about sixty-five years ago."

She frowned and placed a finger on her puckered lips. "That's right. I'd forgotten about that. Bill was a fine man. Always brought the best milk. It was cold too."

Stone bent down to press a kiss to her cheek. "Good morning."

She patted his cheek. "Good morning to you too, dear. Did you decide to get married after all? She's lovely. I can see why you changed your mind," Geraldine said as she smiled at me.

"I didn't change my mind. I'm still not getting married. This is Beulah, the girl I told you about. The one that I think you would like having here to help you with things during the day. Like your hairstyle choices." He added the last bit with a small smile. He had never smiled at me that way.

He was making a joke that only I would get. His eyes sparkled with his smile and made me a little breathless.

"Oh yes, yes! I remember. I was just thinking I'd like to color my hair red. Can she do hair color?"

He chuckled then. A real laugh. It was . . . amazing.

"I like your hair the beautiful shade of platinum it is. Let's not change that."

She sighed. "Very well. I'll leave it like this just for you."

"Thank you," he replied with complete sincerity.

"Do you think you could find where my chickens went? I was going to make some eggs for breakfast," she asked me.

"I—"

"There are no chickens here. That was at your cottage in Bath. You no longer live in England," Stone said to her, stopping me before I agreed to find the chickens.

She waved her hand and laughed. "That's right. Moved last week," she replied. "Come on inside. We'll all catch a cold out here."

She hurried back inside and I noticed one of her shoes was a red house slipper and the other was a white tennis shoe.

Working here would never get boring, I knew that was for sure.

Chapter Eight

GERALDINE LED US into a sitting room with two sofa's that looked like expensive antiques no one should be sitting on and two high back chairs. There was a fireplace made entirely of marble, over it hung a painting of a tall, handsome man with black hair and a square jaw. Although it appeared to be a portrait, it was too perfect to be an actual man.

"There are five guest bedrooms each with an en suite. I have them named and you'll need to memorize them. We will cover that today. The master suite has two en suite's and two sitting rooms. The kitchen is down the hall to the left. The dining room I use daily is across from it. The formal dining room for entertaining or parties is in the right wing further down. It's not proper to have it too close to the kitchen. There is a library, office, bathroom, powder room, sunroom, and this room that need daily dusting, sweeping and the like. I can't keep up with it all anymore. I let the help go after Victor passed because they got in my way." She paused and smiled. "I didn't even offer you tea before I started the job description. I'm terribly sorry. I promise I'm not normally so rude."

"We'd love a cup," Stone replied.

She beamed at us both. "I'll be right back."

I watched as she walked gracefully from the room, baffled by her complete change in character.

"She has her moments. We arrived during one. For the most part, she pretty with it. But the spells as she calls them, come along and she gets lost, confused, forgets, and often thinks it's the 1950's and she's living in England. You'll learn to spot the switch."

"Oh dear heavens! What is on my feet?" we heard her horrified voice from the kitchen. Stone chuckled.

"She'll have to fix that before she comes back."

I laughed. "This is going to be the most interesting job I've ever had."

"Yes, it probably will be."

"How do you know her?" I asked.

He sighed and glanced up at the photo over her mantle. "Gerry's husband Victor was a business associate of my fathers. My mother used to drop me off at my dad's office because I was teething and my crying was too much for her. Granted she had nannies, but they always quit because my mother drove them crazy. Gerry was there one day with Victor when my mother brought me to drop me off. Dad was upset because he had work and she'd run off another nanny. Gerry took me with her that day. Throughout the years they left me with her often. She was the only constant woman in my life from the time I was a baby. The memories I have of my mother are sparse. She came and went, as did my dad's many wives. But Gerry baked cookies with me, took me to the zoo, read to me, taught me how to ride a bike, and stayed by my side at the hospital after my appendix ruptured when I was ten years old. My mother was in Italy with a friend." He stopped speaking as Gerry's footsteps neared.

She was carrying a silver tray with a pretty tea set. "Now, let's drink a spot of tea and discuss your pay."

I watched as Stone smiled at her. There was love in his eyes. This woman was very special to him, and he was trusting me to take care of her. His trust honored me. This wasn't a position he chose just anyone to fill. I understood, and I'd make sure I never let him or Geraldine down.

"There will be times I'm a case I tell you. Be prepared for that," she said as she sat up straight with her legs crossed. I noticed she now had matching black flats on her feet.

"I think she witnessed that already, Gerry," Stone said in an amused drawl.

Geraldine frowned. Then her eyes went wide, and she looked down at her shoes. "Yes, my shoes were a disaster, weren't they?"

"I have meetings today, Gerry. Why don't you and Beulah work things out? You can show her around. Let her get the feel of how you like your day to go. I'm a phone call away if either of you need me," he glanced at me then.

"We will be just fine. Don't you worry about her. I won't scare her away," Geraldine said then winked at me. I liked this woman. My mother would have liked her too.

Stone stood up and sat his cup on the tray then kissed her on the cheek again. "I'll leave her in your care then." His tone was gentle and caring. Who was this man?

"What meetings do you have? Still handling all Jasper's affairs for the boy? It's time you make him figure it out. You've got your empire to run. And Victor's."

Stone gave a hard shake of his head as if to stop her from saying any more. "Everything's under control, Gerry," he said and gave me a tight smile before quickly making his exit.

Handling Jasper's affairs?

"That boy works too much," she said with a sigh. "Do you like to garden? I have a vegetable garden out back. It gives me something to do instead of sitting in this big house all alone every day." The switch in topics was swift, and then she was up out of her chair walking over to the window. "He's a good kid. I often wonder how that's possible with parents like his. He made it out okay though." She glanced back at me. "Can't say the same for Jasper though. That one was stuck with Portia. It ruined him."

Stone wouldn't want her saying any of this to me, but I was clinging to every word. I was finding out more truths every day. My time with Jasper had been brief, and I didn't know as much as I thought I did. I had assumed and judged things that were incorrect. Jasper relied on Stone, not the other way around. Yet Jasper had let me think otherwise. It felt like everything I knew had been centered on lies.

"Now, tell me about yourself Beulah. Beginning with where you got that name. It's Hebrew you know. It means married."

I was impressed that she knew the meaning and origin of my name without looking it up. She was a well-educated woman who had lived what appeared to be an elaborate life. And she was kind. She had been a mother to a little boy whose mother neglected him. That alone made me respect her.

"My mother heard the name on a television show when she was pregnant with me. She was young, and she thought the name was unique and special. She wanted me to be those things, so she said she named me accordingly."

Geraldine smiled. "Well, that sounds nice. She was a good mother then? Even though she was young?"

"The very best in the whole world," I replied without pause. No matter how many lies revolved in and out of my life, my mother's love would always remain the truth.

I understood that she hadn't lied to me about Heidi to hurt me. She'd lied to protect Heidi.

Chapter Nine

CARS WERE EVERYWHERE as I slowly pulled into the small parking lot outside Stone's apartment. There was a single parking spot beside Stone's Rover. That was odd since cars were parked on both sides of the brick-paved road that led to the front of the building. Several were blocking the other cars that parked here regularly.

I pulled into the spot and turned off the car, then heard the sound. It was music and people. Obviously, that's why all the cars came were here. I reached over to grab my purse from the seat beside me and then climbed out of the car. Walking toward the door, I heard more noise and realized it was coming from the roof. Someone was yelling down at me. I heard, "Did we order him some entertainment?" and glanced up to see a guy smiling down at me with a beer bottle in his hand.

The front door was unlocked. I walked inside the building and peeked inside the open door of the first-floor apartment. The people inside were laughing, and there were voices coming from further inside the apartment.

This was very different from the quiet building I'd left earlier today. I had wondered if any of the other people that lived in the building were ever home. I didn't wonder anymore.

A guy with black hair that brushed his shoulders and dark brown eyes walked out the door. His hair was tucked behind his ears and curled slightly near the end. His gaze locked on me and I paused. I wasn't sure if I should introduce myself or just keep walking.

"You must be Beulah," he said as a slow easy grin spread across his angular face.

"Yes," I replied unsure of how he knew that and felt slightly awkward that I had no idea who he was.

"I'm Mack. This is my place. I heard all about you earlier."

"Oh, yes. Stone told me you and Marty live here. It's nice to meet you."

A deep and low laugh was his response, and I wondered if I'd said something funny. I didn't know what that could be. I was trying to be polite.

"When things get too hectic with the crazy bitch upstairs, you're welcome to come hide out here. She hates you. She doesn't have a real reason to, but after seeing you, I think I have that figured out." His tone was friendly.

"Thanks . . . I think," I said not sure if I should agree that Presley was a bit off her mental rocker or not. I decided on going with the truth. "She's got the wrong idea about Stone and me."

That response seemed to please him. "That's good to know. You take care now and don't be a stranger."

I started to say thanks, then thought better of it because it seemed redundant. Instead, I gave him a little wave. Small talk was not my thing.

I continued up the stairs only to find the second-floor door open and more voices and a party inside there as well. Was the entire building having a party? Did these people not have jobs to worry about tomorrow?

I walked up to the third floor quickly before anyone came out of that door to greet me. When I reached the top floor, that door was also open, although the voices weren't as loud and there was no music coming from inside. I didn't know what I was going to face since Presley had already begun sharing her dislike for me with the others in the building. Mack didn't seem to care about her opinion. I hoped the others felt the same.

Stepping inside I saw silver balloons and a Happy Birthday banner across the entrance. Was the entire building celebrating one birthday? I could hear laughter coming from the great room and kitchen, but I didn't feel comfortable asking whose birthday it was. I hadn't been told there would be a party, so I assumed I wasn't invited.

I paused to decide if I should head straight to my temporary room or make an appearance when I saw movement out of the corner of my eye. Looking down the hallway, I found Stone there. He was leaning against the wall with his arms crossed over his chest and his eyes locked on me.

I made my way down the hallway to thank him for my job once again and then maybe he'd tell me what I should do. I was secretly hoping he'd suggest I relax in my room. All these people made me nervous.

"It's someone's birthday I see," I said as I approached him.

He scowled and glanced at the decorations at the entrance

of his apartment. "Unfortunately."

That response didn't surprise me. Stone didn't appear to be the kind of guy to enjoy a birthday party in his space. "I guess you didn't plan this."

He sighed and shifted his eyes back to mine. "Most years I leave the country. Alone. I do something I want to do. Check something off my bucket list. But this year . . . this year I stayed. And Presley did this."

"It's your birthday?" I asked feeling terrible for not knowing. No one had said anything. Not even Geraldine.

"No. My birthday is in two weeks. However, Presley was afraid I would disappear, so she did this early."

I had two weeks to find a gift to thank him for all he had done for me and to wish him happy birthday. I would ask Geraldine for help. She'd know what he liked. I felt bad for him because it appeared Presley didn't care if he'd enjoy a party or not.

"I'm sure she means well," I said trying to remain positive about her.

He raised his eyebrows. "Is that what you really think, Beulah? Or are you just being nice because that's what you do? I'd like to know what you really think. Not what you think you should think."

He was asking for my thoughts. I wasn't sure anyone had ever asked me that. Who would? It wasn't polite to corner someone like that. But it was honest and real, and those were two things I missed lately.

I opened my mouth and readied myself to say what I thought. It wasn't nice but it was correct. Zero sugar coating just as he'd requested. "Presley is selfish and spoiled. She may have some childhood issues I don't know about, but that doesn't excuse her behavior. She had a party because she likes the attention. She isn't worried about anyone but herself." My mouth snapped shut, and I had to fight the urge to cover said mouth in horror. Had I ever said something so incredibly blunt? Without thought to another person's feelings?

Stone grinned. It was that grin that sent my heart rate into a frenzy. "That's better. Sounded real and not rehearsed. I prefer honesty. Brutal, harsh but fucking real. There's enough bullshit in my life."

He pushed off from the wall and came to stand in front of me. His body towered over mine and his scent was a dark and tempting fragrance that made me inhale deeply.

"I trust you. You've got a kind soul. Even when you're honest, it's not cruel. That's rare in my world. You have to know that I won't ever get close to you. I won't ever open up to you. Understand?"

His words had gone from complementary to something else. Did he think I wanted him to get close to me? Had I given off that vibe? Maybe the way he smelled or the way he smiled made me feel lightheaded, but I wasn't pushing myself on him. I wasn't hoping for anything more. I concluded that his comment had insulted me.

"I don't recall asking you to. I've already fallen in love once, and it shattered me. I'm not looking for a replacement." I kept my voice cool and was rather proud of myself for the way I responded.

He leaned down making sure my eyes locked on his. "No, you didn't," he whispered before he straightened and walked down the hall toward his room. I stood there until his bedroom door closed behind him. He didn't turn around to look back at me. He just left me with those last words.

I was angry. I shouldn't feel upset with him. I owed him too much. But his need to be brutally honest wasn't always acceptable. Especially when he didn't know what he was talking about. He couldn't tell me what I felt.

I spun around, walked into my room and closed the door behind me. I locked the door and growled in frustration.

The one thing I hated about his last words? He was forcing me to involuntarily question my feelings. I was asking myself if I had been in love with Jasper. If there had been time for that. In reality, I didn't know Jasper, not really. I had figured out he'd deceived me even if the deceptions weren't that big of a deal. The issue was he had deceived me.

Dropping my purse on the bed, I sank down on the bedspread and fell back to stare at the ceiling. Every moment I had with Jasper had been magical. He'd made me feel a way I never had before. I didn't want to think any of that wasn't real. It had felt real. I wouldn't lose those memories because Stone was cynical. My memories with Jasper were something no one was taking from me.

Chapter Ten

THE NEXT MORNING, I woke up to shouting before my alarm went off. I glanced at the clock—it was only five. Sitting up in bed, I listened. The thick walls and doors muffled most of the shouting. A few words were clear, but I wasn't sure what it was about. Going back to sleep wouldn't be possible now.

My first thought was it was Jasper. He'd come back here to talk to me.

I climbed out of bed and glanced down at my faded pink pajamas my mother had given me for Christmas when I was sixteen. Changing into clothing before I went out there to face whatever was happening seemed silly. I didn't care what anyone thought of my pajamas. Especially Stone. And Jasper had already seen them.

If it was Jasper out there causing a scene at five in the morning, it was time I dealt with him. Stone had been helpful, and he shouldn't have to fight with his best friend over my staying here. Hiding from Jasper forever wasn't going to be possible anyway.

I'd had a full day to get myself together. Life would go on. Heidi was always going to be my sister. And other than the Van Allans paying for her care, they wouldn't be a part of her life.

Opening my door, I took a deep breath to calm my nerves and prepare, then headed down the hallway toward the voices. Stone was demanding that she respect his home. I paused and waited. Maybe I'd been confused. I thought I'd heard two male voices, not Presley's.

"Jesus, Stone, relax. You're always so fucking wound up. She threw you a party. Everyone left late. It'll get cleaned up," the other male said.

"I don't recall asking you what the fuck you thought about it," Stone shot back at him.

"Stop it! Just stop it! Why can't you be nice? You're always so mean!" Presley wailed loudly.

Then there was silence.

I wanted to scurry back to my room, but I'd gotten so close I was afraid they'd hear me if I turned around and walked back. I needed to wait until there was shouting again.

"You live here for free. When your bitch of a mother wanted nothing to do with the spoiled brat she'd raised, I took you in. He didn't. Don't forget that."

"That's an unfair statement. Do you two always fight? I need some fucking caffeine and an aspirin to deal with this," the other voice said.

"Unfair? You were married to her mother. She caught you fucking her daughter and kicked her daughter out. You weren't asked to leave, and you stayed despite the circumstances." Stone's words had my jaw dropping open. Had I just heard that correctly?

"Let it go, Stone! Half the damn country has been married

to her mother!" the other guy shouted back.

"Get out of my house, Wesley. If you want this, then go with him. But don't fucking have a party in my home, trash it, and use it as a way to sneak this bastard under my roof."

"You hurt me with her!" Presley cried.

I waited, covering my mouth in case some other insane bomb was dropped and I ended up gasping out loud. I had to move soon or one of them would come storming out of the great room and find me here.

"She needed somewhere to live. I gave her a place. The same as I did for you."

"And did you fuck her like you did me?" Presley shot back.

There was a sigh. "It was once, Presley. We were drunk. You came onto me naked in the hot tub. I am a man, and you were straddling me rubbing your pussy on my dick. Trust me, I've regretted that lapse in judgment since the moment it happened."

"You're a cold bastard just like your dad," the other man said.

"Says the man who was living off a woman and fucking her daughter behind her back. What happened Wesley? You run out of money, or is it you can't find another brainless female to keep you?"

"Stop it! I can't stay here with you! You're nasty and cruel. I'm going with Wesley. He loved me. He cared about me," Presley said the words as if they were a threat.

I backed up slowly praying no one heard my footsteps. This was not my drama and I shouldn't have heard any of it. Staying here this long had been wrong. I'd been frozen in my spot listening to every word as if it was some television drama unfolding.

"Please, go with him. You have no money. His profession is to live off wealthy women. Good luck with all that," Stone replied and I began to hurry as I tiptoed back down the hallway.

"You don't know him!" Presley yelled.

There was no response.

I slipped back into my room and started to close the door when it stopped just before the latch clicked. A hand was holding it open. My heart quite literally stopped and I bit my bottom lip.

"I trust that answered your curiosity." Stone's voice was businesslike. I didn't have time to decide if he was angry, or if I should respond. His hand was gone and the pressure from my body weight pushed the door closed with a slam.

I jumped back and stared at the door in disbelief. He'd caught me. But he hadn't been upset. At least I didn't think he was upset. That had been rude of me to listen. Intrusive even. I owed him an apology. I could have tried to escape sooner.

A few more doors slammed shut. Presley shouted things. I hurried to the bathroom to take a shower and dress for the day. I'd have to face Stone and apologize at some point.

I needed to think of how to say it though.

As the water ran down over my face, the image of Stone naked in a hot tub popped into my head uninvited and I tried to push it away. I didn't want to think about Stone naked, but the image wouldn't leave. I'd seen him shirtless. I knew how impressive his body was.

Frustrated, I hummed my mother's favorite Elvis Presley song and tried to focus on the lyrics. I tried to picture anything but the image my mind kept displaying. When my body tingled as I unwillingly remembered Stone's description of being straddled naked, I covered my face, horrified by my reaction and thoughts. How was I turned on by that? Was I sick in the head and only now realizing it?

"I am not a sicko, I am not a sicko," I repeated quietly to myself until the water turned cold.

Chapter Eleven

GERALDINE CAME TO the door wearing a red-striped bikini and a large straw hat, carrying around a martini glass full of milk. On one hand, I was a little shocked. On the other, I was grateful she was mindlessly packing for a nonexistent trip to the Caribbean because it helped me drown my thoughts.

I was cleaning up the kitchen after lunch when Geraldine finally came out of her spell.

"Why am I wearing this bikini?" she asked.

I spun around from loading the dishwasher to see her with a towel wrapped around her and her hat was gone.

"You were packing for a trip to the Caribbean," I told her.

She sighed and rolled her eyes. "Dear God, if I ever visit that place again don't let me wear this. My thighs have seen better days."

I smiled. "I thought you looked great in it." I hoped I had her attitude about life when I was older and my brain got scattered.

"Thank you. But trust me. There was a time long ago I could

turn heads," she said with pride.

"I believe you."

She returned my smile. "I guess I have some unpacking to do. If you could water the garden for me while I put things away, that would be wonderful."

"Yes, of course."

She started to leave, then paused and looked at me. "You're a good girl. I've known a lot of beauties. Many that have been in and out of Stone's life. But never have I met one with your spirit or heart. Don't give up on him."

I opened my mouth to tell her that Stone was only helping me and she had the wrong idea about us. However, she had left the room and her footsteps were echoing down the hall before I could gather my words to respond.

Surely Stone had explained our situation to her. He wouldn't want her thinking there was anything between us. Her mind was scattered. Maybe she was confused again thinking I was a girl from his past. That idea saddened me. Stone wasn't an ideal guy to spend your life with. He was hard, blunt and cruel at times. He looked down his nose at others and was closed off. But he also had a soft spot. The idea of a girl hurting him made my heart hurt a little—only a little.

Watering the garden took over an hour. It was an impressive set up and she'd told me yesterday how Stone had helped her organize it during spring break three years ago. They'd spent four days preparing the irrigation and making sure the planting system was installed properly. He would have been a sophomore in college. His friends would have gone to some exotic location to party, but he'd come here to help an elderly woman begin a garden in her multi-million-dollar castle.

Actions like that made the Stone who had told me I hadn't been in love with Jasper seem like a different person. It was as if there were two of him. One I respected and admired, and the other one I wanted to punch in the face.

I wondered how many childhood memories Stone had in this back yard. From the bits and pieces I'd learned about his parents, this must have been his safe place. He came here to be a little boy and feel secure. I'd been raised with love and security. I didn't know what it was like to grow up with parents like his. I couldn't expect him to be normal after that.

"Beulah, dear, we seem to have company. I believe it's more for you than me," Geraldine called from the back patio. When I put the water hose down and looked back at her, the concerned frown she wore made me think she might be having another spell.

"I'll be right there," I assured her and turned off the sprinklers that were set to water most of the crops. She stayed on the patio. Her frown also remained in place. I wondered what she could be imagining to have her so upset. Stone hadn't prepared me for a spell like this. I only knew about her more entertaining episodes.

"Is everything okay?" I asked once I reached her. She sighed heavily as if she hated to tell me what was wrong.

"I'm not sure, to be honest. He's always been welcome here. Because of that, I didn't think one thing about it when he came to the gate. I happily let him inside. I was ready to make him a cup of tea and feed him a slice of the almond pound cake you made earlier. But when he got inside the house, he asked to see you and I remembered. Stone warned me this could happen and said I should tell you to call him if he tried to get in here. But . . . I forgot, and now he's here. In the parlor."

"Jasper," it wasn't a question. Although she had never said his name, I knew who she was referring to. He shouldn't have come to my job. To a place that he'd always been welcomed. It was wrong to take advantage of Geraldine. Instead of the panicked mess I'd been every time I thought I'd have to face him, this time I was angry. I was frustrated that he'd do something like and that he'd upset Geraldine.

Facing him was the last thing I wanted to do, but I wouldn't allow this to upset her more than she was. "That's all right. Not to worry. I'll see if I can help him then send him on his way. Or you can feed him some pound cake and enjoy your tea. I'm sure he'd like that."

She shook her head. "Oh, no. He isn't to stay here with you. Stone told me to be sure this didn't happen, and I messed it up."

The distress in her voice was unfair to her. Jasper was being selfish. "Then you have a seat in the kitchen, and let me handle Jasper. This isn't a problem at all and Stone doesn't even need to know about it."

Geraldine pinched her lips and shook her head. "No, no. I'll have to tell him. And you're not going in there alone. Stone didn't tell me why, but he was very adamant about it. I just wish I'd remembered sooner."

Arguing with her was a waste of time.

"If you're sure," I said worrying this was too much stress for her.

She gave a firm nod. "Absolutely."

I didn't know what he'd say or why he was here, but I had to deal with this and make him leave. Coming between him and Stone's friendship made me feel terrible. Jasper and Stone were as close as brothers. It wasn't until after I'd left that I realized how close they were. Stone and Jasper didn't have a lot of family from what I could tell, and they weren't going to lose each other over me.

"Then let's go see what our guest wants," I said with a smile that wasn't genuine.

She studied me then sighed. "This isn't good," she muttered. "Let's go."

With Geraldine by my side, we walked to the parlor, and I began mentally coaching myself to face him. I had to do this without any crack or breakdown for Geraldine's sake. Maybe for my sake too.

When we got to the doorway, Geraldine stepped in front of me almost protectively. "I brought her, but you're not supposed to be here. I had forgotten. So I won't be leaving you alone. Stone didn't give me any details on the situation and I know you boys are close. If he thinks that you shouldn't be around Beulah, then there must be a good reason."

Jasper's eyes weren't on Geraldine, they were locked on me. My chest ached at the sight of him. I was surprised it wasn't as painful as I'd feared. I didn't care what Stone said, I loved Jasper. Or I had. The way I'd felt for him had changed. My feelings had to change with the truth. He was a Van Allan and my sister's biological brother. I wasn't bitter that my sister didn't have the privileged life Jasper had because she'd been given something so much better. I felt sorry that he had to grow up with those monsters as his parents.

"Stone won't allow me in the building. You won't answer my calls or texts. I didn't know how else to talk to you." The pleading in his voice was hard to disregard.

"Stone is trying to protect you. You have to accept the truth and admit the lies, then maybe we can talk. Right now, it's too fresh, too painful."

Jasper took one step toward me, and Geraldine took a step toward him as a silent warning. She didn't seem to care that Jasper was a foot taller than her. She held her head high and glared at him with determination.

"Gerry, you know I won't hurt her. I just need to talk to her."

Geraldine shook her head. "You're talking, but you're not getting closer. I wasn't supposed to let you inside."

Jasper lifted his eyes to look me. "I want a DNA test for Heidi. And I'm having one done for me too. I . . . Hell, I don't know what my parents were capable of. If Stone is right . . . Jesus, I could be a bastard of one of my father's secretaries. I need to know the truth. I can't just accept what Stone believes is true. God knows my mother can't tell the truth. She is still protecting herself. She always will."

Heidi didn't need her DNA tested. It would scare her or confuse her. I shook my head no. "I won't have Heidi upset."

He took another step in my direction. "She won't ever know. We need a swab from inside her mouth and a strand of hair. Nothing else. If she is a Van Allan, then she deserves the inheritance that is rightfully hers."

"No! She is an Edwards. My mother," I felt emotion clog my throat making it hard to speak. "My mother . . . was our mother and she always will be. Heidi needs to know nothing more than that. I WILL NOT let you upset her! Nothing is more important than Heidi." I was speaking loudly, my heart pounding in my chest for other reasons than the sight of Jasper. It was fear that I couldn't protect Heidi if she was a Van Allan.

"I would never, ever, hurt her. She would never have to know anything more than she does now. But . . . I'd like permission to visit her. If she is my sister, then I've missed out on that. I never had a sibling. I want to know mine."

My throat was closing, and my hands felt sweaty. I shook my head and backed away from him. Panic was causing my vision to blur. This wasn't happening. If I had no claim on her, if they found out she wasn't my sister . . . I could lose her. They could take her away from me. They'd be able to whisk her off to wherever they wanted, and she'd need me. She'd be scared and confused.

I couldn't breathe. I couldn't breathe.

Chapter Twelve

BEFORE I HAD a complete panic attack, the front door swung open.

"JASPER!" Stone's roar echoed through the house. I jumped, jerking my head around to see him taking long quick strides into the parlor with a furious expression. I'd never seen him show this kind of emotion. For a moment, I snapped out of the complete breakdown I was having over my sister.

His gaze swung to me, and his expression softened. "Are you okay?" he asked his tone still harsh.

I managed to nod because I wasn't sure if I was okay, and I was afraid to tell him otherwise.

"No, she's very upset. She wasn't even breathing. It's all my fault. I let him in. I forgot. I thought he'd come to visit me," Geraldine was upset and I had failed at keeping her calm. I'd forgotten about my determination to keep this easy and harmless for her sake when he'd said he wanted to test Heidi's DNA.

My breathing hitched again reminding me what could happen. How easily my world could be taken away. Heidi was all I had.

"Jesus, you've gone white," Stone said as he walked to me in three quick strides and studied me. His fierce expression wasn't enough to stop my tears from welling in my eyes.

"Out! Now! OUTSIDE!" Stone roared again as he turned toward Jasper. He advancing toward Jasper so swiftly I was afraid of what he was going to do.

Jasper didn't argue, but he met Stone's glare with one of his own as he stalked past him and headed toward the front doors. Stone touched Geraldine's shoulder. "Thank you for calling me. None of this is your fault. I'm sorry he brought this to your home." His tone was tender.

She shook her head and looked at me. "No, no, no, I should have remembered. I should have—"

"You did exactly what you should have done," he assured her then glanced at me. "Take Beulah and get her some tea. She'll be okay. She's tough."

It was as if he was talking to me instead of her. I even nodded in agreement. I would be okay. I could do this. I wasn't going to crack.

He must have needed that assurance. A slight nod confirmed he agreed, then he left us there and followed where Jasper had exited. I watched him go, each of his strides had purpose. Jasper wasn't weak nor was he small. They were similar in size. But something about Stone was more intimidating. He was harder than Jasper and had darker thoughts. As if the survival instinct was stronger in him than other people. I wondered if his childhood had something to do with that.

"Jasper should have expected that," Geraldine said with a

shake of her head like she was disappointed in his choices. "Come now, honey. Let's have some tea. It's good to calm the nerves. Your pretty complexion has gone pale."

I let Geraldine lead me back to the kitchen, but I felt guilty. This wasn't Stone's battle. "I should go out there and talk to them. He and Jasper are too close."

Geraldine laughed then. It was an amused sound, and she continued to chuckle as she walked into the kitchen. "Sit," she ordered me with a point of her finger toward the table. "Stone can handle this. Jasper came to my home when he knew better. This is Stone's issue to handle, not yours. You need some distance. From what I hear you're dealing with family issues that are terribly upsetting. I imagine the Van Allans have done something awful. And from the conversation I overheard just now," she paused and looked at me with the teapot in her hand, "that baby girl of theirs didn't die." She appeared to be waiting on my confirmation. I couldn't respond. If Geraldine knew about Heidi's real identity then who else remembered the baby the Van Allans buried?

She frowned. "The worst kind. Only the worst could do something like that," her voice was just above a whisper.

"She's the best person I know," I blurted out suddenly needing Geraldine to know Heidi was nothing like her parents.

"The way you love her is a testament of that. Tell me. What was it that they were displeased about to give the child away in such a deceptive way?"

Stone trusted Geraldine. She obviously knew the Van Allans and had for a long time if she remembered Heidi's birth. This was hopefully going to become my job. I'd be here for years to come with her.

"Heidi has Down syndrome," I said knowing eventually

Geraldine would find out anyway.

She nodded. "I should have guessed as much when you spoke about her before. That kind of beautiful soul quite often comes from such a child. I'm glad that the mother you loved so dearly was hers as well. Portia Van Allan is a," she grimaced and said, "bad seed."

"She's my mother's sister," I explained.

Geraldine stared at me a moment before her expression softened. "Two sisters so completely opposite. The way I see it is God gave the world two beautiful girls and wanted them raised by a woman worthy for them to call mom. Heidi was meant to be with your mother. In your heart and Heidi's, she always will be. No matter what the Van Allans choose to do or say."

She turned to make our tea and I stared at her back feeling some peace from her words. Geraldine was a unique lady. I wanted to get up and hug her and thank her for saying that. For listening to me. For giving me this job.

She spun around with a surprised look on her face. "The Christmas tree delivery should be today! I haven't even made the cider yet. Do you think we can string some popcorn next? I don't want to have an empty tree. Victor will need to get the ornaments from the attic. I have antiques you know—my mother had beautiful ornaments that are hand blown. Exquisite I tell you. Glorious. You'll have to handle them with care. But you'll see," she continued to ramble on as she left the tea forgotten on the counter and went to begin looking in the pantry for cider supplies.

"We have nothing! I'm not ready for the holidays at all! Claudia will need to take me to town. What is a tree without the smell of cranberry tart in the oven?" she sounded panicked as she ran from the kitchen.

I jumped up and went after her unsure of where she was going next.

The large front door swung open, and Stone came walking in with a scowl on his face. He stopped short when he saw Geraldine coming his way in a hurry. "Oh Stone! You're here. Good, good, you can get the ornaments. They're in the attic where we packed them away last year. The tree will be here soon. Claudia is taking me to get the cider and cranberry tart supplies in town. We will be festive in no time! Just you wait and see!" She clapped her hands and did a little hop.

Stone's eyes lifted from her to me. "It seems it's December," he drawled.

I nodded.

"Are you okay?" he asked.

"Yes. I've got it together now. I'm sorry I cracked."

He didn't appear pleased by my response. "Jasper won't be back. There will be no DNA testing."

The sigh I released gave me great comfort. "Thank you."

"When you're ready to talk to him, let me know."

"Okay."

"Come on Claudia, dear, we've got to get to town," Geraldine said as she spun in circles looking for something. "Where is the coat rack? I had one just there by the door. We can't go out in that weather without our coats, scarves, and hats." She was getting distressed again.

"Gerry, it's the end of July and ninety degrees out there. You don't need a coat, nor do you need to go to town for cider."

She looked confused. "Oh. I guess I should tell Claudia," she muttered and turned to walk away. When she turned into the library, Stone shifted his gaze to me. "Claudia passed away of cancer in 1983. She was her younger sister."

I glanced back at the door she'd disappeared into. "Will she remember that?" I asked him.

"Not until she comes back around. I never remind her that Claudia and Victor are gone when she's in that state. There's no point. She remembers a happier time, one she misses."

Chapter Thirteen

AFTER ALL THAT had happened today, I'd almost forgotten about my eavesdropping when I shouldn't have been that morning. Making up all the excuses in the world for why I stood there and listened to the fight between Presley, Stone and the Wesley guy was pointless. I knew the truth. I had wanted to understand Stone and Presley's relationship. I'd expected more than what the actual truth was. I shouldn't have been so nosey but I had to admit I was relieved.

Thinking too much about why I was relieved was uncomfortable though. I didn't want to do that. Jasper was enough to keep me upset and awake at night. I didn't need to add more to it. I could ignore the curiosity I had with Stone.

Stone's vehicle was parked outside but Presley's was now gone. Knowing I was going to walk into the apartment without her there was nice. She made me tense. I imagined she made most people tense, men and women alike. The girl was over the top.

As I made it to the second floor the door to the apartment there opened, and a tall, willowy brunette stepped out. She was everything you saw on the face of beauty and fashion ads, commercials, and billboards. Exotic, perfectly placed features was the only way to describe her face. She yawned as if she was just waking up at seven in the evening. The tiny shorts and crop top she was wearing were the kind you'd see on a runner. Her hair was pulled up high in a ponytail. The unique color of her green eyes focused on me and she paused.

"Thanks," she said and then propped her incredibly long leg up on the wall and began to stretch.

"Excuse me?" I replied completely confused.

She glanced at me then touched her nose to her knee. "I'm thanking you. You are Beulah Edwards correct?"

I paused. Then nodded before realizing she wasn't looking at me to see my response. "Yes," I verbalized.

She switched legs and continued the stretching. "You got the crazy bitch out of here. We all owe you thanks. I'm just giving you mine."

I didn't know if this was Chantel or Fiona, but I knew they were the two that leased this apartment from Stone. I was good at remembering names. I'd just never met either of them. I'd also assumed they were friends with Presley the way she had talked about them the first day I arrived.

"I didn't do anything, it was Stone. They argued," I explained deciding if it was rude to ask who she was since she obviously knew who I was.

The girl dropped her leg and then began bending her waist with her hands over her head. This time looking directly at me. "They had arguments, fights, fucking loud ass screaming many times. But this is the first time she packed her shit and left. You're here. That makes this your doing. Claim it as a victory. We all credit you."

I didn't know who "all" referred to. I also didn't have a thing to do with Presley's leaving. Unless you take into account that she thought I was sleeping with Stone. But lots of women had slept with Stone. I shouldn't have been the one that sent her packing. Especially since I had not, in fact, slept with Stone.

The door behind her swung open and a familiar face that took me a moment to place appeared. "Do you have tampons?" she asked her gaze swinging from the girl to me. She straightened and took a step out the door as the recognition slowly came on her face. She pointed. "Jasper's maid," she said her eyes wide.

"Jesus, Shay. Fucking rude," the girl muttered. "This is the one who got rid of Presley."

Shay's eyes began to smile as her mouth joined in. "No shit! I knew I liked you. Not that we talked very much. I had on no pants, it was early, and I was hungover and late for work. Great party though."

"Ignore my little sister. She's not the best with words," the girl tossed her ponytail back over her shoulder and gave me a bored look that I imagined made her money. "I'm Fiona. This is Shay my sister and a regular house crasher."

Shay rolled her eyes. "Not that I like crashing here. The two of you don't eat actual food. I'd starve if it weren't for Marty and Mack."

"Whatever. I need to run," Fiona's tone was slightly annoyed.

"Why? Did you eat too many carrots today? God knows you need to run that shit off."

"Stop being a dick. Wouldn't hurt you to get in a run. The

cookies and chips you've been eating aren't doing you any favors," Fiona called out as she ran down the stairs.

Shay flicked her middle finger up. "Skinny bitch!"

I stayed paused. Unsure if it was polite to leave now.

Shay smirked at me. "Same dad. Not the same mom. My mother was a farm girl from Virginia. Fiona's mother, on the other hand, was an heiress from Spain. Our father likes them beautiful. And young. Once they hit thirty-five he shops for a new one. Anyway, that's why she looks like that and I look like this," she said waving her hand over her body. "Oh, and the cookies and chips. She's right about those."

This world I was now involved in seemed to be overrun with fathers who married often and young. I was starting to understand more and more why my mother didn't marry. She was smart.

"I'd offer you food, but they seriously have nothing unless you consider kale, lemon, and quinoa food. And I haven't got a clue how to cook that quinoa shit. But I was about to go down to Mack and Marty's. They have the best snacks. Marty brings home fresh donuts from the place by the fire station he works at."

A fireman. Interesting. I hadn't met Marty, but I had met Mack. If Marty was a fireman, then Mack had to do something that made money. I didn't imagine a fireman could afford the lease on this place with his salary.

"I ate before I left work, thank you. It was nice to see you again," I replied.

She nodded. "Yeah. Same. Thanks for getting rid of the bitch. She was insane. I don't live here, but I'm here enough to dread seeing her. I caught her with Dan in his study one afternoon when I first started working for the Elswoods. I never said anything, but I haven't been a fan of hers since. Claire isn't the warmest or most likable woman on the earth or in a room of ten people, but no one deserves to be cheated on. I keep my distance from Dan," she grinned. "Anyway, too much info I'm sure. Have a good night. I need to get sustenance before I pass out."

"Yeah you too," I replied awkwardly as she jogged down the stairs toward the guy's apartment.

This place was like living in a television drama.

Chapter Fourteen

I KNEW I could come and go as I pleased at the apartment. It was my temporary home for now. It was difficult to get comfortable because it felt like I was intruding on Stone's personal space. I decided I'd walk inside quietly and go to my room. After all, he needed to enjoy the peace he could with Presley gone.

What I didn't expect was for the place to smell like garlic, butter, and heaven as I stepped inside. Closing the door softly behind me, I glanced toward the kitchen and heard classic rock on the sound system and noise that could only mean someone was cooking. I wasn't shocked that Stone could cook. Jasper had mentioned his culinary talent once. However, witnessing him doing something so domestic was surprising. As curious as I was, I wasn't going to walk in there to see him in action for myself. He needed personal space, especially after the day he'd had.

I turned and headed down the hallway just as Lynyrd Skynyrd's "Free Bird" started playing. I liked his taste in music. If the entire house was going to have this music playing, it was an enjoyable choice.

As my hand touched the knob on the door and I was just about to turn it to make my escape into my room, his voice stopped me. "It's rude not to say hello. Especially when someone is cooking dinner for you."

I released the door handle and glanced back at him. He was standing at the end of the hallway wearing a white apron tied around his waist, a black cotton short-sleeved shirt, and jeans. His tanned bare feet completed the image. My words faltered as I stared at him. He didn't seem upset, and his expression wasn't as dark as it normally was. The tension in his shoulders was absent. He was relaxed, and that was as out of place as it was attractive. Maybe attractive wasn't a strong enough word. He was striking, breathtaking, much like Fiona had been in her running gear. The difference was my heart hadn't stuttered at the sight of her. If it had, I might be in less of a predicament.

"I didn't know you were cooking for me. I thought . . . you were celebrating your peaceful house tonight."

His laugh was short and he sounded amused. "Oh, I am. But I don't bother to cook pierogi for myself. That shit's too damn hard."

I had no idea what pierogi was, but it smelled delicious. I'd made a tomato mozzarella salad with grilled chicken for dinner at Geraldine's. We'd sat on the back patio and enjoyed our meal while she told me stories of Stone and Jasper's childhood. The happy kind of stories. The ones that made us laugh. She had also given me some ideas for Stone's birthday.

However, I wasn't going to tell him I'd eaten. This week alone, Stone had helped me and saved me over and over again. I could eat a second dinner if that's what he wanted. Heck, if he asked me to walk a tightrope from this building to the next I would have a hard time telling him no. I would of course tell him no because I had a recurring dream of falling from a tightrope to my death. The recurring dream started after watching a news report when I was a child about that exact thing happening to a lady at the local circus.

"Thank you. I should be the one cooking you dinner though. You had a rough morning then you had to deal with the situation at Geraldine's. I am causing problems for you. I don't want to do that."

He wiped his right hand on the apron that hung on his waist. "Jasper is my best friend. I've been pulling him out of shit since we were kids. I'm the harder one. He's emotional, and I'm not. Today wasn't about you, it was about him. This . . . is about him," Stone said staring at me. His gaze locked on mine. "Don't feel as if you owe me anything. Except to eat the meal I slaved over." He finished his last sentence with a softer almost teasing lilt to his voice.

I didn't want to think about the seriousness of his words. I'd come to expect Stone's brutal honesty. But allowing myself to give in to his attractive qualities—the way his eyes lit when he smiled, or the security I felt with him—was dangerous. He was protecting Jasper. Believing any of this was for me would only hurt me in the end.

Right now, I was weak, broken, and my heart was longing for a way to heal. Stone was not offering open arms nor should I be leaning his direction for sympathy. Even if this was all for Jasper, I was thankful for his help and I owed him my gratitude. Eating dinner twice was a small price to pay.

"Thank you for making dinner," I replied simply. Saying more was needless. He had said all that needed to be said.

"You're welcome. You gave me a reason to cook. I've missed it."

Jasper had given him a reason to cook. That thought popped up so quickly it almost sounded bitter in my head. I put a hand on that thought mentally and squished it down. I was not that girl. I never had been, and I wouldn't start now. Stone wasn't mine, and he wasn't meant to be mine. My confusion was because I felt such strong feelings for Jasper. My emotions were blurring the lines, confusing things.

"Get comfortable. It'll be a few more minutes. Dinner here isn't a formal thing. I'm barefoot, and the table out on the balcony won't have a tablecloth on it. Wear whatever you want."

With that, he walked back to the kitchen. I waited until he was gone before letting out a sigh. From day one Stone had made me uncomfortable, nervous, and angry. The relief, gratefulness, and odd flutter in my chest at the sight of him now mixed with those other emotions was making this all too much. If I could just stop that damn flutter. If I didn't take him in like I was drinking a cold drink of water on a hot day when I saw him, this would all be easy to deal with. I was good at adjusting. I was a fighter. But this . . . this was different. Fighting my attraction for a man I did not want to be attracted to was not one of my strengths apparently.

My common sense said he was Jasper's best friend and that alone made him out of my reach. Stone wasn't the kind of man a woman should fall for—not in love, or lust because he did in fact lack emotion. Unless he was looking at Geraldine. Or when he allowed his stepsister to drive him crazy because she had no home. Or when he stepped in time and time again to save Jasper from causing himself any pain or harm. Other than that . . . he was hard.

Frowning at my train of thought, I went into the bedroom and dropped my purse on the bed before changing into a pair of black leggings and a large gray sweatshirt that said Ireland across the front in green. I'd bought it for one dollar at a thrift store three years ago. It was soft and worn. When I felt lost inside, I cuddled in its warmth.

Leaving my feet bare I made my way toward the kitchen. The music had been turned off, and the only sounds in the apartment came from the activity in the kitchen.

Stepping inside the kitchen, my gaze immediately went to Stone. He was filling a plate with what looked like a pasta dumpling and salad. His gaze lifted to mine and a pleased smile touched his lips. "I think it turned out good. I'll let you be the judge of that though. Haven't made these in a few years. They were one of Gerry's favorite when I was a kid. She taught me to make them."

Again, when he said her name I could hear the love clearly in his voice. I couldn't say Stone was always unfeeling and hard as his name suggested because the way he felt for that elderly woman dismissed his grumpy demeanor.

"It looks delicious," I assured him. It also smelled delicious.

"You ever had pierogi?" he asked setting one plate down and picking up the second one. His eyes were still on me.

"No," I admitted.

"Good," he said as he finished preparing the plate. "You won't have anything to compare it to. Less pressure on me."

"If they taste as good as they smell I'm sure it'll be wonderful. Can I help you do something?"

"Wine. I usually have a chardonnay with pierogi carbonara. A sauvignon blanc is good too. But stay away from reds. Never enjoyed the combination."

I had no idea how to choose wine. Even when I was told what kind to choose. They were all the same to me. But I didn't say as much. Instead, I went to the large wine rack beside his bar and looked for either of the two wines he mentioned. I figured I'd go with the first I found. Different wineries meant little to me.

Glancing at the wines, I only saw reds. Then I remembered that the Van Allans kept their whites in a wine cooler thing. I checked for one and found it behind what appeared to be an elaborate cabinet door. The chilled white wines lined the racks inside. I quickly found a chardonnay, pulled it out and met Stone in the doorway. Both his hands were full. "Glasses and wine opener are already on the table. Take it out there. I'm right behind you."

I started to turn when his eyes went to the bottle and he chuckled.

I glanced at the bottle wondering what I'd done that was amusing. When he didn't say anything else, I looked at him. "What's wrong? You did say chardonnay?" I began wondering if I'd misunderstood.

"Yes. I did. And you chose the cheapest bottle. It also happens to be my favorite. I've never had a female pick that bottle out. Most go for the Montrachet or the Coche-Dury Corton-Charlemagne."

He could have been speaking a different language for all that meant to me. I could act like I knew wines or be honest. He knew my background and pretending in front of him was silly. "I just grabbed the first chardonnay I found."

He chuckled some more. "Well, you'd have found five more bottles of the one you're holding right now. I buy a bottle every time I go to Target."

Target? Stone went to Target? "Really?" I asked wondering

if he was making a joke.

"Yes. They are the only place around here I've seen it. I try to grab a bottle when I'm close by."

The idea of Stone shopping at Target made me grin. That seemed so out of place.

"Something funny?" he asked.

I nodded. "Yes. You shopping at Target. Sorry, but that's funny."

He smirked then. "I like the soft pretzels in their café there too. Want to laugh about that while you're at it?"

I did. I laughed loudly. I didn't mean to but I did. Stone with a Target soft pretzel was too much. When I finally gained composure, I wiped at the tears in my eyes and smiled up at him. He was watching me. His expression was one I couldn't read and was so brief, it was there for a moment then gone. I almost thought I didn't see it, but it had caused a flutter. Damn that flutter.

Chapter Fifteen

THE TASTE OF the crisp cool wine felt nice on my tongue. It washed down the delicious meal perfectly. Stone explained the filled dumplings were popular in Eastern Europe. He also told me about the process to make them. Geraldine had been taught by a Polish friend of hers when she was a young woman. I ate and listened to him talk. As the wine relaxed me the sound of Stone's voice became richer, thicker, and more appealing.

That was not a good thing. I knew it, and I fought against it until my third glass of wine made me simply not care. It wasn't my fault Stone had a nice voice. I had to accept it and get on with my life. Right now, I would enjoy listening to him talk though. It wasn't hurting anyone.

Once the food was cleared from my plate and my third glass was almost empty, the pain that came with thoughts of Jasper was gone as was my constant fear of losing my sister. I trusted Stone. He said I wouldn't lose her and I believed him. I had no reason to think he was being dishonest. He was a good man. He was a bastard at times too. But deep down he was good.

"No I'm not, Beulah," he replied.

I frowned wondering what he was talking about. Had I said something out loud? "Huh?" I asked needing clarification.

"Deep down I am the same. Cold, hard, indifferent. Don't confuse my actions for anything more."

I had said it out loud. He didn't mention the bastard bit, so I apparently hadn't said that. Words continued to pour forth without my bidding. "I disagree. I've seen you with Geraldine. I know you have a heart. You protect her and care for her. You give her that smile that other women never receive. Then there is the way you protect Jasper from himself. You have your problems, but no one helps you or seems to care."

I snapped my mouth shut realizing I was saying way too much and the wine was the reason.

"They need me. I don't need them. I don't need anyone."

"Everyone needs someone," I replied.

"No, Beulah. They don't. Some of us are strong enough."

No one was strong enough to need no one. "You need to be needed. You need Geraldine and Jasper to need you. That's what gives you peace. It gives you purpose. Maybe you aren't weak by needing to be rescued the traditional way. But you need to be strong. That's what saves you."

As I heard the words coming out of my mouth, I understood him better. Strange how a little Target wine can make you see things you were missing.

Stone stood up and picked up both of our plates. "I believe that's enough for us both. Good night, Beulah. I hope you enjoyed dinner and sleep well," Stone said as he walked inside with the empty plates. I stared at the door as it closed behind him. My butt was still planted firmly in the chair. I had made a very good observation and he'd walked off. Just like that. Had it angered him? Why did he get to say whatever he wanted and then walk off when something he didn't like was said?

Was he not allowed to have a weakness? Even if he needed to be strong for someone else? It was still a need. We all had needs.

I stood up quickly shoving my chair back as I did it. My balance was off somewhat but I ignored that. I had a mission. I was going to tell Stone just that.

The kitchen was my destination and I stalked toward it with determination. Storming inside my expression fierce. Ready to make Stone hear me I had barely gotten inside when I said loudly. "It is human to need something. You are a human. Needing to be needed is ALLOWED!" I finished that with my hands firmly planted on my hips as I managed to focus on Stone.

He was at the sink on the other side of the counter where he had been rinsing off dishes. We stood there. His eyes locked on mine. No one said a word and the time felt as if it was slowly ticking by and Stone was never going to speak. But his gaze held me there. Immobile. Worried I should have just gone to bed and not been so determined to prove a point. The dang wine. One glass would have been plenty.

Just when I began to think we would stand there all night in this staring contest waiting for the other to break, he moved. He walked around the bar and stalked toward me. I didn't think he was going to hurt me, although the scowl on his face concerned me the closer he got to me.

When I thought he would walk right past me still scowling, he stopped inches from our bodies touching. I inhaled sharply, preparing for whatever hard and possibly cruel things he was about to let loose.

"You're right. It's human to need. It's part of our flaw. Or weakness," he began. His voice was deep and dark. I shivered but didn't want to move away. "But that's not a fucking need. It's part of my life. A part I accepted a long time ago. I need. Yes. I need something I cannot have. That's what I need, Beulah. What I need and want is mine are two different things."

His words were like a riddle but he smelled so nice and the heat from his body was so close I didn't care at the moment. He could keep speaking in riddles, I would keep listening.

Stone closed even more of the tiny bit of space left between us. "Right now, I need you to go to your room and lock your door." His tone was threatening, and I shivered again.

He leaned in until his mouth was at my ear. I closed my eyes and took him in. His presence. His strength. His scent. "Go to your motherfucking room. Now." Although his words weren't a shout. They were a demand. I pulled back and looked up at him. He closed his eyes tightly. "I have asked little of you, Beulah. Do this one fucking thing for me. Please."

Those were the words that sent me to my room. The words I couldn't argue with because he had done so much for me. He had asked for nothing from me. He was always there to save the people around him. So instead of pushing, waiting, or hoping for the unnamed, I backed away until I was far enough from him I could tear my eyes off his almost black ones and walk to my room. As I moved away from Stone, my heart pounded faster, and my need to escape was clear.

The unknown was there nipping at my heels. The threat of something that would break me unlike anything else was too close. I knew I had to flee to save myself.

Chapter Sixteen

STONE WASN'T HOME when I woke up. I had listened for him as I got ready for work, but heard nothing. The smell of coffee didn't linger from the kitchen. When I walked out of my room, I noticed his bedroom door stood open. I didn't have to look inside to know his room was empty.

I didn't go to the kitchen or look anywhere else for him, but I did stand at the door and wait in case he was lurking somewhere and decided to show himself. After several silent minutes, I opened the door and left the apartment.

Drinking three glasses of wine had been a terrible idea. I never drank because I was a lightweight. I remembered everything, but I worried that my memory was hindered from the alcohol. Had I offended him, or worse, said something embarrassing? Something embarrassing, like my thoughts out loud. My attraction to Stone wasn't going to be welcomed by him. It's possible he'd hate me for it. I only knew of two people in this world he loved unconditionally. Geraldine and Jasper.

I glanced at the closed door on the second floor and thought about how I'd assumed the wrong things about the girls living there. In my head, they were all like Presley. I found it shallow of Stone, and I might have judged him for having women like her surrounding him. I knew differently now.

When I reached the bottom floor, I saw Mack wiping his face with a towel. He was sweaty and dressed in running shorts and a T-shirt that was soaked. A bottle of water sat empty on the floor beside him. Did everyone who lived here run? Was I the only one without an exercise plan?

He looked over at me and frowned, then smiled slowly. "You must be, Beulah. I think I'm the last one to meet you."

He didn't remember meeting me. That was either embarrassing for both of us or he was drunk that night and I hadn't realized.

"Oh," I said thinking of how to straighten this out. "Um, well, we did meet. The night of the party that Presley threw for Stone." I wasn't sure if that was rude or not, but acting like we hadn't met seemed silly.

He chuckled. "No. I'd remember meeting you. A guy doesn't forget that face. You met Mack. I'm Marty. Except for the birthmark on my left calf in the shape of a warped looking heart we're identical. We tried changing our appearance over the years to make ourselves look different, but we outgrew it. No more piercings, weird hair colors, or glasses that aren't needed. We just accept that we look alike and go with it. But I'm the smarter one. So there's that."

Identical. Wow. I studied him a moment and didn't see anything that differentiated his appearance from his brother. Maybe if I were around them more I would find a distinguishing factor.

The entry door opened and in came Fiona with a to-go coffee in her hands. She was wearing high-heeled boots that came to her knees and a skirt that was barely covered her bottom. She looked like she'd just done a photo shoot for a magazine.

"Good morning, Beulah. Marty," she said knowing exactly which brother was standing in front of us. She had no problem telling them apart. There must be some trick.

"Morning," he said less enthusiastically without sparing her more than a glance.

"Good morning," I replied.

She smirked. "Be careful with him." Then she headed up the stairs.

I glanced at him and said nothing. I tried to think of a way to end the conversation now that Fiona had just made it awkward.

"She hates me, ignore her," he said grinning as if that was normal and okay.

"You fucked someone else when we were dating," she called from the second floor.

My eyes widened in shock. I really wanted out of this conversation.

"We were on a break! Jesus, Fiona. Let it go!"

"I was in Italy you bastard. Our break didn't mean we could fuck other people!" She then slammed the door and I stood there wishing I hadn't witnessed their argument.

He sighed. "It was a year ago. I had asked her to marry me. She said she needed space and went to Italy for work. I took it as she was breaking up with me. I got smashed and slept with an ex-girlfriend. But hey, I was honest with her about it. I told her the truth. She didn't take it well."

I nodded. "Obviously."

He chuckled. "Old news. Anyway, it was nice to meet you. Don't be a stranger. Shay, Fiona's sister, hangs out with us often. The door's always open."

"Thanks," I said glancing at the door. "I need to go. I'll be late for work."

He was still grinning when he said, "Have a good one."

"You too," I replied then hurried out the door and to my car.

Stone's Rover wasn't there. I pondered where he'd gone. Was he hiding at Jasper's pool house again? This time it was from me instead of Presley. I didn't want to run him out of his home.

It was peaceful here with her gone. My presence in his home shouldn't keep him from enjoying his peace. If it did, I would find somewhere else to live. I was making good money with Geraldine. I shouldn't continue living with him anyway. I'd talk to him about it tonight.

The drive to Geraldine's was short, but my thoughts bounced from Stone and last night, to Jasper at Geraldine's yesterday, to Heidi and the fact I needed to visit her. This week had been too busy adjusting to it all. I had only called Heidi three times, grabbing time to speak with her while Geraldine napped. During our last telephone call, I'd promised yellow and pink cupcakes on my Sunday visit. I needed to get to the store for the ingredients and attempt to make them in Stone's kitchen.

I rolled up to the gate and buzzed Geraldine.

"Hello," came her voice over the speaker.

"It's Beulah," I told her.

"Oh good! You must be here with the Chinese food I ordered. You know it's been three hours. You need to work harder to make your delivery times." The speaker cut off abruptly and the gate opened.

My morning was going to start off interesting. Maybe when Geraldine came back around I could ask if she wanted to make cupcakes with me and join me for a surprise visit with Heidi later this afternoon. Geraldine needed an outing.

Stone issues would have to wait until tonight. I would deal with it then. Jasper issues would never be gone. My focus needed to stay on Heidi. I also had to find my way in the world and move on. Thinking about anything more was a waste of time. Being attracted to Jasper had led to all kinds of pain. I didn't need to add more to it by letting myself feel something for Stone.

My mother had a perfectly happy life without a man.

I could too.

Chapter Seventeen

IT WAS ALMOST time for lunch when Geraldine's mind was back in the present. Before that occurred, she thought she was living in New York City and was engaged. I wasn't sure what year that had been, but she was happy and excited about her wedding. She was also very upset I wasn't the Chinese delivery driver. She had wanted eggrolls and orange chicken.

"Do you feel like going out today? I was thinking I could make some cupcakes and we could visit my sister."

Geraldine was cleaning the makeup off her face that she'd applied earlier to attend a ball with her fiancé. She paused and smiled. "That would be lovely. I've heard so many things about Heidi. Meeting her would be a treat."

Relieved that she liked the idea, I glanced at the pantry. She was stocked with everything needed for baking. "Could I use your supplies to make the cupcakes? I'll restock all the items I use. It would save me some time."

Geraldine waved her hand at me. "Don't be silly! You use whatever you need. I'll help. It will be fun. I don't have much of a reason to make cupcakes anymore. Let me get the mixer and measuring cups. You get whatever you need from the pantry." She clapped her hands together excitedly.

This job was more than I could have hoped for. Geraldine was such a good woman—in her right mind and out of it. My job was just another thing I owed Stone. I often felt like I didn't do enough to warrant the paycheck. Geraldine was good company and there was never a boring moment.

Once we had all the ingredients on the counter we began working together. Geraldine said she was best with the cake batter if I could do the icing. I was fine with that. I had a special way of making the icing that Heidi loved. The pantry was filled with so many sprinkles to choose from I had a hard time deciding, but ended up choosing the glitter-like sprinkles. Heidi would be amazed at how they shimmered on the pink and yellow icing.

While we were finishing up, I decided to ask Geraldine's opinion on the best way to handle moving out of Stone's. I would admit I had become attracted to him. That was something I'd deal with and end myself. Telling someone made it harder to ignore.

"I think Stone would enjoy his apartment without me there. With Presley gone he has the opportunity to have it all to himself." I stopped myself from saying more. I wanted to see how she responded first.

"If you're thinking of moving out, I think you'll have a fight on your hands. Stone will worry. He wants to keep you safe. Having you at his apartment gives him reassurance that you're okay."

I wasn't sure I agreed with that.

"He's helped me so much already. I'm thankful for all he's

done. I don't think I can ever repay him."

She starting placing the finished cupcakes on a pretty pink platter. "He helps the people he wants to help. When he is sure you're ready to move on he'll make sure you have a home to move to. He's a good boy."

This wasn't how I had hoped this conversation would go. "He is helping me because of Jasper. I shouldn't be his burden. It's not fair. Jasper and I will never be. He needs to have time to work and be there for Jasper. It's what he wants."

Geraldine looked up at me then. "Saving Jasper's ass isn't what he wants. He feels it's his job. The boy has so much responsibility he piles on himself. Always has. But he wants to help you. Since he came in here the first time and told me about you he has been different. When he talks about you he seems . . . different. Like a bit of his darkness is gone."

Although that sounded good, she saw things very differently than I did. Stone was crystal clear that he was helping me for Jasper's sake. "Stone was less dark when he told you about me because Jasper and I were over. He was worried about Jasper and I having a relationship. He knew the truth or suspected it."

Geraldine pressed her lips together and almost smirked at my response. "The first time he told me about you was the weekend after he saw you the first time. So that reasoning of yours is incorrect. Now," she dusted her hands off on her apron. "These cupcakes are finished, and I'm anxious to meet Heidi. Enough of this. Let's go."

I stood there mentally going over what she'd just said. I thought I must have heard her incorrectly. Stone wouldn't have spoken about me after he met me unless it was to complain about my existence.

"Stop frowning. It causes wrinkles. I'll get my purse and we can be on our way."

"He hated the sight of me," I told her.

She was confused. That was the only explanation.

Geraldine laughed then. A loud amused sound that made her eyes twinkle with delight. "Stone has never once hated you," she managed to say through her laughter.

I realized talking to her about this was a bad idea. She got times and facts wrong all the time. I went to pick up the tray of cupcakes and smiled. "I'll take these to the car."

"Get my keys from the washroom. We will take my car," she said still smiling like she was trying to stifle more laughter.

I headed toward the washroom to get the keys I had seen hanging in there. Taking Geraldine to see Heidi might not be a good idea. She could forget what decade it was at any moment. It appeared that she might be close to having a spell now. Then again, Heidi wouldn't realize there was an issue.

The idea of my sister listening to Geraldine's ramblings with interest made me smile. She'd buy the madness, and ask questions. When I walked back into the kitchen, Geraldine was there with her black flats on her feet.

"She's the closest thing to an angel I've ever seen," Geraldine said when she saw me.

"Who?" I asked thinking she may be lost again in her memories.

"He will never see more than that though. In her eyes, there is more. I want to see it all and know those secrets that made her so strong. But I won't get the chance. I saw the way he looked at her."

That wasn't an answer. It was more rambling. "Do you know where we are going?" I asked to see if she was with me still.

She smiled softly. "Yes, Beulah. We're taking these cupcakes and visiting Heidi."

Okay, so she was still sane. "Oh. Then what were you talking about?"

"I was remembering that first conversation I had with Stone about you."

Chapter Eighteen

HEIDI WAS THRILLED we visited. The glittery cupcakes had been a big hit. She'd been happy that I'd brought my new friend.

Geraldine's mind stayed in the present the entire visit. She had shown Heidi a trick to crochet, played kickball with us, and pushed Heidi on the swing she loved under the big oak tree.

It wasn't until we arrived back at Geraldine's that she started talking about me priming the water pump and checking on the chickens. I let her ramble on and fixed dinner while she ran around the house cleaning for the make-believe company she was having. Her sister would be at this party and she needed to make sure the linens were freshly pressed. By the time I convinced her she needed to have dinner because there wasn't a party tonight, she came back around and I was able to leave at the normal time.

Stone's Rover wasn't there when I pulled up to the apartment. Sighing, I sat in the car and stared at the building. I was forcing him to stay away. Last night's wine had given me a loose tongue, and now he wouldn't come home because I was here. Geraldine had said things that made me question what I thought for a moment. But she was wrong. Stone didn't want me around.

A knock on my window caused me to jump in my seat and I jerked my head to the left to find Mack or Marty standing there with a grin. I wasn't sure which one it was now that I had met them both.

I rolled down my window instead of opening my door. I wasn't sure I'd be going inside tonight. I needed to think things through first.

"You gonna sit out here all night?" he asked.

I shrugged. "Not sure yet."

My response turned his easy smile into a concerned frown. "Why? Stone being his moody self?"

I glanced back at the building. "No. I just think I've outstayed my welcome."

"You've hardly been here. Stone's a good guy, but he can go bastard really easy. Ignore it. He wants you here. Besides, you got rid of Presley. You're like a motherfucking super hero."

I knew he was being funny and trying to get me to smile, but I couldn't manage one.

"Come on. Marty is grilling steaks. I'm about to make some of my famous broccoli salad and Shay promised she would bring a peanut butter pie from Hannah's Sweets down the street. We need help eating all that."

This was Mack. I hadn't been sure until he talked about his brother just now. How did anyone tell these two apart?

"I don't have anything to bring. I can't come empty-handed."

He chuckled. "Yeah, you can. Shay is only picking up the pie because I said she needed to bring something since she eats here all the damn time. And I wanted some of that pie. Hannah's is on her way home."

I glanced back at the building and thought of going up to Stone's empty apartment. Right now, he and Geraldine were all I had apart from Heidi. It wouldn't hurt me to make new friends.

"Okay, thank you. That sounds nice."

I had eaten with Geraldine, but here I was eating a second dinner. I was going to gain weight doing this. One thing was for sure though, I would not be drinking wine tonight.

I rolled my window back up and opened my car door. Mack stepped back to let me out, waiting for me. I picked up my purse and locked the car door. He walked beside me toward the front entrance.

"It's quieter around here with Presley gone. Thanks for that," he said breaking the silence.

"Yes, it is. But I didn't really do anything. She decided to leave." Why they were all so sure it was me that sent her running I didn't understand.

"You're living under his roof. That was all she needed to go insane. Well, she was already insane. You only pushed her over the cliff. Figuratively speaking. However, if you do push her off a real cliff give me a call. I'll help you hide the body."

I paused and stared up at him in horror.

He started laughing and patted me on the back. "Ease up there, beautiful. It was a joke."

I relaxed and started walking again.

"How did you meet Stone? Rumor is you're his friend, uh, what the guy's name?"

"Jasper," I said wishing he wasn't asking me about this but

he'd been so nice I couldn't be rude.

"Yeah, Jasper. Met him once. He doesn't come here much. Anyway, the chatter among the girls was you're his ex. Seems unlikely though since those two are so tight. I can't see why he'd be giving his buddy's ex a place to live."

He opened the door for me to enter and I went inside. I was regretting agreeing to dinner now. There was no way I could explain this and still be vague.

"If I'm being nosy, tell me to stop asking questions," he said sounding as if he felt bad about asking.

"It's not that . . . it's just a very long and confusing story. One I don't want to share. I'd rather forget."

He gave me a nod of understanding. Then stepped in front of me to open the door to his apartment. I heard country music playing and the smell of bacon drifted to me as we walked inside.

"Brought company! You got on clothes?" Mack called out loudly.

The idea of Marty with no clothes on made me blush as I couldn't help but imagine what that might look like.

Marty stepped out of an open doorway into the entry room. He was wearing a pair of jeans and a navy-blue T-shirt that said US Marines on it. A large spoon was in his hand and his face broke into a grin. "Beulah! Damn that's a relief. Sometimes he shows up with women that annoy the hell out of me all night."

"Whatever. You fucking loved Layla," Mack said dropping the gym bag he'd been carrying on the floor beside the door.

Marty shrugged. "Yeah, well, it was easier to ignore the annoying shit when her profession was dancing on a pole."

Mack chuckled and Marty winked at me like I was in on this joke. I didn't have much to add to this conversation but I didn't want to appear as if I were a prude either. I could be one of the guys. I went with the first thing that came to my mind.

"Our neighbor growing up was an adult dancer. She was a single mom putting herself through college. After she got her nursing degree, she stopped dancing. She also started eating a lot of bread. She was always bringing us a loaf."

I was rambling about a lady I hadn't thought of in a very long time. Her daughter Melanie was three years younger than me and ended up getting pregnant at fifteen and running away. I wondered what had happened to both of them.

"Got to love a stripper with a goal. Bet that bread packed some weight on her," Mack said walking toward Marty and what I assumed was the kitchen.

It had. She'd gained about thirty pounds the first year she was a nurse. I didn't mention that.

"Enough about the beauty of naked women dancing. Come try the bacon wrapped mushrooms I just took off the grill. They're fucking delicious," Marty said waving me toward him.

I followed them both into the kitchen and saw what could only be described as cooking destruction. There were open cabinets, spilled ingredients and even some splatters of what looked like sauce all over the place. I paused mid-step and looked around the room in horror. What in the world had happened?

Mack glanced back at me holding a toothpick stuck in a bacon wrapped mushroom. "Try it. He's right. It's fantastic."

I continued to stare at the mess he'd made.

"Marty isn't a clean cook. You'll get used to it. He can't seem to create anything without a disaster around him."

I managed a nod like that made sense, but honestly, I had never seen such havoc created from simply cooking. "Is that . . . a slice of onion on the fridge door?" I asked still trying to take in the wrecked kitchen.

Marty glanced back and laughed. "Yeah. Guess it is. Not sure how I managed that."

"He cooks and cleans this shit up. If I had to clean up, I'd eat out every night," Mack said as he popped another mushroom into his mouth.

"A masterpiece can't be produced in structure. Chaos. It takes Chaos," Marty said.

Mack rolled his eyes and asked me, "You want a beer?"

"No, thank you," I replied.

"She's not a beer drinker. Look at her. She's got the wine look. A rosé wine. Am I right?" Marty asked.

I enjoyed rosé or wine in general, but I wasn't touching any wine. Not again. "Water would be good."

Marty opened the fridge, took a bottle out and handed it to me. "Water it is. But those steaks would be good with a glass of red."

The door slammed, and seconds later Shay came strolling in with three bakery boxes in her hands.

"Those don't say Hannah's on them," Mack said sounding annoyed.

Shay sighed. "That's because they aren't from Hannah's. The Elswoods had a dinner party last night and so much shit was left over. I have a variety of delicious sweets. You will eat them and be happy."

"Dammit, Shay. I wanted that pie."

"This was free. Suck it up, eat the expensive free sweets I brought and be happy. Some celebrity chef made this stuff."

Mack stalked to the fridge and jerked it open, then took a

beer out and opened it. "I don't know why we put up with you. You can't even bring me the damn pie I want."

Shay sat the boxes down. "Because I'm lovable and you can't live without my witty jokes."

He snarled. "Fuck that," he mumbled as he turned to look at me. "She's why I drink. I swear."

It was odd. But I felt chemistry burning off both of them. I wondered if they even realized it. There was a definite attraction between the two. They might not want it, but it was there. I shifted my eyes to Marty who was watching me. He winked again and smirked. Like we shared a secret. He saw it too. Hanging out tonight might be just the thing to get my mind off my life. I would certainly enjoy watching this drama unfold in front of me.

Chapter Nineteen

"CAN I SAY that I'm glad you're who Mack brought to dinner tonight and not another mindless bimbo," Shay said opening the third box she had brought as she placed it on the table.

We had finished the meal. It had, in fact, been delicious. Marty might make a huge mess but he was a talented cook.

"They aren't mindless. Ask Beulah. She had a neighbor who was a stripper that needed to put herself through college and take care of her kid," Mack shot back at her.

"Yes. Well, that kind of stripper isn't the kind you bring home. The last one thought that chocolate milk came from brown cows," Shay said before putting a chocolate tart in her mouth and glared right at him as if she dared him to explain that.

"She was kidding," he muttered.

"No, brother. I believe she was serious. She also didn't know Hillary Clinton was once the First Lady. She had no idea who

Bill Clinton was," Marty reminded him. "But she did look good in the dress she had on, so I can understand why you missed her lack of common sense."

Mack let out an annoyed huff as he reached to slide one of the boxes across the table. As he peeked inside he said, "In her defense, she was two his last year as president."

Shay began to laugh as if that was hilarious. Tears filled her eyes and she wiped them as she still laughed.

"God, would you stop it!" Mack barked at her.

She covered her mouth trying to stop. Marty was grinning too. "Dude. We didn't know she was only eighteen. I'd have kept that to myself."

Mack shoved a cookie in his mouth and looked angry.

"Dinner was great," I told them. "Can I help clean up the kitchen?" Hopefully, my subtle change the subject would lead them away from discussing Mack's horrendous choice of females.

"Both of you are running off Beulah. Can't y'all shut the hell up?" Mack said as he stood up with another cookie in his hand. "Sorry about them. But no. You don't touch the kitchen. That's his job. If he needs to destroy it then he can clean it. Or Shay can help him since she didn't manage to bring me the one thing I asked for."

"You're enjoying those cookies just fine," she snapped at him.

He held up both hands as if he was done with her. "Because that's all we fucking have!"

Marty sighed then turned his head to me. "It's a damn circus around here."

Today had been a long day. I wanted to talk to Stone and make a decision. But leaving without being rude would be tricky. I didn't want them to think I was leaving because they were fighting.

Because honestly, it was keeping me distracted.

"You can go. No harm done. I'd leave if I didn't live here," Marty said. I started to explain when a loud knock on the door stopped me. It also stopped Mack and Shay's fighting. Or more like their argument.

"I'll get it," Mack said and stalked from the room.

"He's such an ass," Shay muttered.

"Mmmmhmmm," Marty replied but he was grinning like he didn't believe her. I had to agree with him. She almost seemed to be enjoying the constant word battle with Mack. Like she had not brought the pie on purpose.

"It's for Beulah," Mack called and I stood quickly at the sound of my name.

"Stone must be looking for you," Marty said as he stood up too.

Would he come here looking for me? It seemed unlikely. I folded the napkin I'd had in my lap, then dropped it on my used plate before leaving them there and going toward the door. I figured when he got home and he saw my car out front he'd be curious. But he could have called. My phone was in my purse, completely dead. I'd forgotten to charge it last night. I blame the alcohol—I was drunk.

When I walked into the entryway and saw him standing there, his eyes locked on me. Pausing, I wondered if I should explain or apologize. Did he even care? Had he tried to call?

"You're not answering your phone," he said sounding angry.

"We were loud—" Mack had started to make excuses for me but I interrupted.

"I forgot to charge it last night. It's dead."

Stone held my gaze a moment longer. His expression was

unreadable. I couldn't tell if he was angry, concerned, or annoyed.

"You weren't home when I got here. And—"

"I asked her to have dinner with us. I'm sick of Shay and Marty. Needed to change it up a bit," Mack explained for me before I could say more. I glanced at Mack and he seemed relaxed. "There's plenty left if you want to come in. Shay brought some expensive ass shit for dessert from the Elswoods."

Stone shifted his focus back to me. "Are you finished?"

I nodded. But I was nervous. Unsure of his mood. I didn't say anymore.

"I've already eaten," he said to Mack. "But thanks for the offer."

"Anytime," Mack replied then turned to look at me. "Glad you could come tonight. You're always welcome."

"Even more welcome if I bring the peanut butter pie," I said with a smile.

He chuckled. "Yes. Anyone is welcome if they come with that in hand. Fuck knows Shay isn't gonna get one."

"Goodnight," Stone said abruptly as he opened the door and then looked at me as if I were supposed to move first. So I did. I thanked Mack again as I left the apartment with Stone following at my heels. The door closed behind him. I kept walking toward the stairs. There was tension and I didn't understand why. Did he not like Mack and Marty? Was there a problem with me having dinner with them?

I didn't ask.

Instead, I waited. Stone would tell me when he was ready.

When we reached the top of the stairs, I paused as he stepped around me and unlocked the door. He waved his hand for me to go inside first. I did.

The lights came on as we walked inside and I scrambled for the right words to say. If I'd just come up here when I got home I would have had time to prepare my thoughts. I couldn't find the right words because I was nervous and unsure of how to broach the subject of last night.

"Goodnight," Stone said simply then headed down the hallway to his bedroom. I stood there speechless as I watched him leave me standing there. He'd come to get me as if we needed to talk. But he was going to bed? Seriously?

"You came to get me to make me go to bed?" I asked unable to stop myself.

He stopped walking and stood there a few moments before turning back to me. "No. I came to get you because you're naïve. Mack is a known womanizer. He's not like Jasper. He's a professional at using women."

With that explanation, he continued on. Before I could think of something else to say or formulate more questions to ask, he was gone. His door closed firmly behind him.

And I was left alone. We hadn't discussed anything. Not about me leaving or how long I should stay here. Nothing.

Chapter Twenty

FOR THE NEXT week, Stone wasn't home when I left for work in the morning and when I got home in the evening. Geraldine had even asked about him. Wondering why he hadn't been by to visit. She'd asked if I had decided on his birthday gift. I hadn't. I feared my moving out may be the gift he wanted.

She and I went to visit Heidi three times that week. I had kept busy trying not to worry about Stone's disappearance and what my possible role was. I laid awake at night listening for him to return. Anxious as to what I would say if he did.

Seven days after my last interaction with Stone, I pulled into a parking spot in front of the apartments and found Jasper standing there. His hands were tucked in his front pockets. His head was down. His shoulders were slumped slightly as if he were defeated.

The sight of him made my chest hurt. I didn't like seeing him like this. With him out of sight, I was able to block out my fear that he would take Heidi from me. That she was technically his sister, not mine. He could be considered the villain in my story.

Seeing him there, however, made that impossible. He was kind and good. Nothing like his parents. He'd been a victim as much as Heidi had. His parents had lied to everyone. Heidi would never know or understand their actions, but Jasper did. He had to live with that knowledge.

I turned off my car and got out. His head lifted to meet my gaze. He seemed broken. The gleam of playfulness in his eyes was gone. His easy smile that once made my heart race was no longer there. He seemed older. The easygoing guy I'd fallen in love with was gone.

I stepped onto the sidewalk and stood there. I was several feet away, waiting for him to explain why he had come. I wondered at the same time if I should have gotten out of the car. Our last confrontation hadn't gone well and Stone wasn't here to run interference. Was I strong enough to handle speaking to him alone?

"I'm not going to pursue finding out the truth about Heidi. You're right. She had a mother. A family. You're her family. You're what she knows and loves. My need to prove the truth will just cause more pain," his voice sounded sad. Empty.

"Thank you," I replied with relief. The weight on my chest lifted. I'd been living with that fear since the moment this all began unraveling with Portia's lies.

"I won't be back. I leave for Manhattan tomorrow. My things are already set up in my place there. I'll be running things from the main office. Away from this town, Portia, and," he paused. Closed his eyes tightly and exhaled. "You."

That should have stung. But it didn't. With Jasper here, I always lived with the fear I'd have to face him one day. Or see him with another girl. I wasn't sure how I'd feel watching him move on with his life. Which was what we both had to do. There could never be an us.

"What about your Savannah office?" I asked because I didn't know what to say. I had no idea what response to give that wouldn't hurt us. It was impossible to know what to say that would make this end and we could both walk away.

"It was a waste of time. I have enough to handle with my father gone. I need to focus on what was already built. Being here was . . . something I wanted once. Portia's lies and the truth I have to face daily in this town makes it the last place I want to be."

He could start over somewhere else. Make a new life. A life I wouldn't have to witness by accident when I ran into him some day in town. His moving away made it easier for me to let go of the memories. To heal from the lies.

"You'll be happy there. This will become the past and you can forget it all," I finally said.

A sad smile barely tugged on his lips. "Yeah. Sure."

"Thank you for everything, Jasper. For being there when I needed someone. For paying for Heidi's care. You have been more than I could have asked for."

A frown creased his brow. I didn't know what I'd said that had upset him, or what was causing him to study me with a confused look.

"I didn't pay for Heidi's care. I was going to, but I forgot. With all this shit going on, I never got around to it. I'll do it today. I want to do it."

He was still talking, apologizing. I didn't hear his words though. They were muffled by the pounding in my head. The knowledge that I knew was there. The truth. And what that meant. I shook my head trying to grasp the reasons behind this. If what

I thought were indeed true.

When I realized he wasn't talking anymore I focused on him. "You never paid it?" I asked for confirmation.

"No. But I will, I swear. I won't leave that on you," he replied. His expression determined yet apologetic.

"It's paid. You don't need to," I said the words before I could think about it. Before I could weigh if it was the right decision to share that knowledge with him.

He tensed. His shoulders straightened. His back went rigid. The hardness in his expression wasn't directed at me, but the way his eyes changed I knew he was fighting a mixture of emotions. Anger being the first one while a flurry of others danced vividly with every breath he took.

He stepped past me and started for his car.

"Goodbye, Jasper," I said wishing this hadn't been our last conversation.

He opened the door to his car and inhaled deeply before swinging his gaze back to look at me. "You'll need me one day. When that day comes, call me."

Then he was gone. His car door closed and he pulled away from the apartments. He left with nothing more than those dark words that I knew he meant as a warning. I stood there for a long time after he was gone. I thought about him, all that we had said, and Stone. It always led back to Stone. The answers seemed to have been there the entire time, yet I had missed it.

The payment for Heidi's care had been made by him. I didn't have to ask him. It made sense. The payment had come moments after I left him there on the street while I had been falling apart. He'd told me that Jasper had sent the payment. He'd even paid it in the Van Allan name. He'd wanted no credit and nothing from me in return.

Why? That couldn't have been for Jasper's sake. Could it? If so, wouldn't he have just reminded Jasper? Asked Jasper to pay him back? The home Heidi lived in cost a small fortune.

"Hey!" a male voice called behind me and I turned.

Mack or Marty was standing at the entrance of the building waving me inside. "Come eat with us. Stone won't be back for days. When he leaves for the Manhattan offices it's always a week at least."

Manhattan? He was out of town? When had he left? Had he been gone all this time? My emotions were so tangled, I couldn't face anyone right now. Especially Mack and Marty. I needed to be alone.

"Thanks, but I'm exhausted. I'm going to bed early," I told him hoping my smile looked sincere and not like the grimace that reflected the turmoil inside.

"You gotta eat," he shot back.

"I ate with Geraldine. Today's been a long one."

He sighed then nodded. "Okay. Are you coming inside?"

There was no reason to stand out here waiting for no one. I walked toward him and he opened the door wider, allowing me to pass him to enter the building.

"The guy. He upset you?"

I turned to look up at Mack or Marty and saw the look in his eyes. This was Marty. The flirty gleam that was always in Mack's eyes wasn't ever present in Marty's.

"That was closure," I told him.

He studied me a moment, but didn't ask anything else. He simply nodded and patted my shoulder. "Go enjoy the quiet. Tomorrow will look brighter."

I hoped he was right. I didn't see how that was possible.

Chapter Twenty-One

MY EYES FLEW open. The darkness from outside was still casting the moonlight through my window and across my room. Reaching for my phone, I saw it was only two in the morning. I'd only been asleep for three hours. Sitting up, I looked around to see if something had woken me. I'd been dreaming, but in my dream, there had been a sound. One that made me pause and wake up.

I was on the top floor of a very secure building. Someone breaking in was incredibly unlikely. And even if an intruder broke into the building, Mack and Marty would have heard and intercepted them on the ground floor. I felt safe here, but I was sure a sound had woken me.

Footsteps in the hallway wasn't what I expected to hear next. Jumping out of bed, I hurried to the bedroom door and swung it open without thinking who it might be or if I should be calling for help. I'd always been the one to go charging head first at danger to protect Heidi. It was instinct that drove me.

None of that mattered because it was Stone who stood in the dark hallway. I was relieved. It was highly unlikely someone had broken in, I just wasn't expecting him back for a few days according to Marty.

"You're home," I said as our eyes met.

"Yes," his reply was deep. As if he'd been sleeping. Which he couldn't have since he'd just arrived. Or at least I thought he had.

"I didn't know you went out of town until today." Why I said that, I don't know. He was returning home and here I was pushing him. I feared he'd leave again. I wanted to cover my mouth, and run and hide in the room.

"I needed to think," he said still watching me. He was searching for something in my eyes, my expression—I wasn't sure. I felt almost naked from his intense perusal. Exposed.

"Did you?" I asked him. My voice was a little to breathless. I realized my heart was pounding. All this from his scrutinizing stare?

"Did you?" He threw my words back at me.

"Did I what?" I was confused by the path the conversation had taken.

He took a step closer to me. "Did you think?"

Did I think? About leaving? Getting my own place? About the stupidity of too much wine? Yes. I thought about all that. But I didn't know what he meant. "Did I think about what?"

"Me."

My breathing had become a little labored and erratic. But the tone of his voice when he said that one word made it stop completely. My body tensed. The darkness didn't mask the uncertainty in his eyes. He was asking even though I could see he was scared of the truth. I'd never seen fear in Stone's eyes before. Not until this moment. It was almost humbling.

"Yes." Saying anything else would have been a lie.

He swallowed hard, inhaled deeply through his nose and seemed to be internally battling his next move. My hands trembled and I gripped them together in front of me Neither of us spoke. The silence made me uneasy.

Each breath we took seemed louder and more dramatic than they actually were. I knew the thoughts running through our heads—the facts, lies, and the truths—made this all harder and simple all at once.

Even though my heart raced, my body tingled, and my hands seemed incapable of being still, I knew that the one truth wouldn't let this moment be anything more than it was. Stone loved Jasper as if they were brothers. If by some chance that display of emotion I'd never seen in his eyes or in his actions were what my heart wanted it to be, it wouldn't matter. Because attraction did not outweigh love.

That reminder helped me calm down. To get caught up in this moment had been weak and a mistake. I could be hurt again. No, I would be hurt again if I thought there was a chance at more with Stone. A chance to know the man that I had misjudged, misunderstood, and disliked so fiercely.

Stepping back into the bedroom I reached for the door to close it. I wanted this to end . . . whatever it was.

"He came here before he left," Stone said stopping me.

I just nodded.

"And he still left. Closed the Savannah office and left," he said this as if it were important.

I nodded again. A brief nod. No need for more.

Stone closed the space between us until I had to tilt my head back to see his face, his eyes. I searched his expression, attempting to understand him. My heart was once again beating as if his nearness shot jolts of electricity through it. Why did Stone have to cause such a reaction in my most important organ?

"A man that deserved you. That understood what you are and what he had. What he had lost. He wouldn't leave. Even if it were an impossibility to hold you again. He'd want to protect you. Even if he couldn't have you. If his having you meant pain to others. Even if his motherfucking chest felt like it might explode from the sight of you. He wouldn't leave because he wouldn't be able to. Your security, protection, happiness would be all he could focus on. The only way he could survive."

When he said it that way, in those brutally blunt words, I realized he was right. Jasper's love for me wasn't what it should have been. Love meant never leaving, never running. It meant you could never be too far away. To be fair, I'd done all three to him. The pain and loss had faded quickly enough. What I'd thought was a shattered soul had only been a bruised heart.

"We hadn't known each other that long," I said in both of our defense. I couldn't blame Jasper when I'd run first.

His mouth almost formed a scowl. "If it's real, does that matter?"

I thought it did. Love wasn't instant. True love came from knowing someone. "Love takes time, yes. You need to earn respect, find out the things the other enjoys, laugh together. If love is forever, how can it happen without time?"

The tips of Stone's fingers brushed my cheek as he ran one fingertip along my jawline. I shivered and fought the urge to lean into him. Standing here with him didn't seem real. It was more like a dream. A fantasy. The kind of fantasies I was having more often while trying to shove them away from me.

"You were wearing that damn uniform Portia gave you. Your hair was pulled up in a ponytail. The elastic band holding it up was black and slightly frayed. I wondered if it was the only one you had and if it was near breaking. There was a slight stain on the collar but it was pin size. You wore no makeup except for lip gloss—it was pale pink. But that was all you needed," he paused and looked down at my bare feet. "You had a slight limp. Nothing too noticeable, but it was there. I wondered if it was permanent. It didn't take away from your beauty. Nothing could," he lifted his gaze back to mine.

"You worked for a monster like Portia. I'd thought you'd wanted the job because you knew about Jasper Van Allan. Just for a moment, I watched you closely, quietly, and finally saw your eyes. There was stress, pain, anxiety, but most of all, fear marring their beauty. That moment. When our eyes met and I saw you. Not the outward appearance, but your soul that you shared so clearly in your eyes if someone took the time to look, I knew I would love you. There was sadness inside you I wanted to heal and fear I wanted to erase. Pain I wanted to ease." He stopped and held my chin. Not harshly but with pressure to tilt my head back further as his dark eyes melded with mine. "I began to investigate, to search, to protect you. Understand that, Beulah. I did it all to protect . . . you."

Chapter Twenty-Two
STONE

THINGS HAPPEN IN the blink of an eye. Death, life, and sickness are all things that changed our lives. From the time we are born, we learn to expect the inevitable end. We fear it, anticipate it, and learn to live with the outcome. However, until I walked into the Van Allan kitchen and my eyes locked on Beulah for the first time, I'd never realized there was one more thing that could happen in a split second. Was it love? I can't say that it was. Calling it attraction was too weak of a description. I was drawn to her. As if an invisible thread was pulling at me.

Then I'd seen the look in Jasper's eyes. He'd been instantly attracted. He fought his attraction because his hate for Portia made him want to hate anything connected to her, and she'd also hired Beulah. As much as he wished that he couldn't stand her, that he could be cruel to her, he couldn't take his eyes off her. She couldn't stop looking at him either. I read people well. I often knew what they felt before they did. It was easy when you didn't need to speak. Staying silent and observing left one to study things others missed.

I held myself back. Waited. Hoped that she saw just how different Jasper was from her. Not his money or wealth, that wasn't the issue. She was strong where he was weak. She had been raised by a woman who had given her courage, self-worth, and an appreciation for the things often overlooked. Jasper hadn't. He was still similar to a boy. He leaned on me for more than I should have allowed. Yet he'd been my family for most of my life. It had always been Geraldine and Jasper. The only two who I knew were there for me.

I wanted to believe my words. I wanted my diligence in finding the truth about Beulah and Heidi to have been for Jasper. Telling myself I was doing it for him eased the guilt when I searched harder, pushed past barriers in my way, and broke a few laws. The truth was, deep down I knew the entire time I was doing it because of her. Part to protect her from unseen pain and danger. Part to make sure she wasn't being taken advantage of. And lastly to prove my gut was right. The Van Allan's had a secret. One that would make her and Jasper an impossibility. That was my darkness. I'd wanted her so damn bad, Jasper hadn't been my concern.

He didn't deserve Beulah. She didn't know him. She thought he was someone he wasn't and he led her to believe that. My jealousy began to build disgust from his lies.

The guilt I should feel for having Beulah here with me never came. Even when Jasper accused me of the truth—wanting her. I didn't feel guilty because I wanted her to heal and for her heart to realize it wasn't love she felt for Jasper. I had waited for her. Given her the time she needed.

When her eyes began to look at me differently, I knew I

couldn't ignore that pull inside me. The hunger to touch her, inhale her, to be free to hold her.

Jasper leaving was it the last step. He was leaving. Running. If I had a doubt about his feelings for her this made it clear it wasn't enough. A man that walked away from Beulah didn't deserve her.

My time of quietly living in torture was over.

Lowering my head until my mouth covered hers for the first time was as close to a spiritual moment as I'd ever experience. The air around us stilled. Her breathing stopped. My heartbeat pounded steadily in my ears. The heat from her lips seared me and I knew it was me trembling from the connection.

Beulah's left hand reached up and covered mine as I caressed her neck. My right hand slid around her waist applying pressure until we were pressed together from head to toe. Every inch of her body touched mine. She leaned in with complete trust. My kiss hadn't scared or surprised her. She'd responded with the same urgency I had rushing through me.

I wanted to look into her eyes and tell her everything. To explain it all to her. But not now. She didn't require it. Like me, she seemed to have been waiting. Anticipating this moment.

Pressing my thumb against the pulse in her neck, I felt the rapid beat that matched my own. My right hand slid down to cover her perfectly round bottom. I squeezed gently and a moan escaped her as she shifted closer, spreading her legs slightly. The subtle invitation made my already hard dick throb. This moment was one I had imagined, planned, fantasized over. I wanted to take my time memorizing every kiss, sound, and expression in her eyes.

What I wanted and reality were beginning to become two different things. The build up from the moment I saw her. The moment she spoke. The moment that damn smile squeezed my chest, it had all brought me to this.

She lifted a knee and slid it up my leg until it was at my hip. Another invitation. Grabbing her thigh, I growled in frustration. My hunger for her was growing out of control quickly. With more force than I intended I squeezed her thigh and jerked her legs open wider and pressed my erection as close to her center as I could. She wasn't tall enough to give us the heated connection we were both craving. With both hands, I grabbed her waist and pulled her higher.

Without instruction, she wrapped her legs around me. My cock was pressing against her where she pulsed with excitement from the connection. The warmth between her legs cradled me and made my knees slightly weak. It felt as if an animal had broken free inside me causing any softness and gentleness I possessed to fade.

"AH!" Beulah cried out as her head fell backward and she lifted her hips then lowered them to rub my hardness against her aching clit. She grabbed my shoulders with both hands, her eyes closed tightly and she began grinding against me.

"Uh, oh, oh," she panted. Her body moved with eagerness for more.

I wasn't a religious man, but watching her I began to understand devotion. Her voracious response was stirring my lust. I'd dreamed I'd worship her. Now I wanted to own her. Lose myself inside her. Reach a level I knew I'd never been. One that would change me as much as the woman in my arms had.

Unable to stand still any longer as she pleasured us both with her moans and pure abandon, I moved toward the bed. Quickly. Every ounce of blood in my body felt as if it were moving to my growing erection. It was more sensitive than it had ever been. I couldn't wait. I couldn't take my time. Not anymore. My desire was controlling my actions.

I pressed her into the bed, pulling back to shove her legs apart. Her eyes were hooded and her chest rose and fell as if she were out of breath. "I was going to take my time." My voice sounded like a growl. The crazed animalistic need had taken over. "But you rubbed that sweet pussy on me." I lowered my voice and bent down to press a kiss to the exposed skin beneath her ear. "Your reaction made me snap," I added.

Pulling back, I looked into her eyes to see if I'd frightened her. But all I saw was excitement. A craving that matched my own. My hands were still on her inner thighs. Holding them open as wide as they would go. I reached up and hooked my fingers in the waist of the pajama shorts she was wearing. "When I take these off and see just how wet you are, smell how fucking sweet your desire is, I'm afraid I will lose any small portion of control I still have left."

I was warning her. Even now when my body was literally shaking with my desperation for her. I was giving her a chance to stop me.

"Good," the soft challenge came out in a breathless pant.

If there was any thread of sanity left in me, it vanished with that single response.

Chapter Twenty-Three
BEULAH

IN ONE BRIEF moment, it crossed my mind that this was another me. This wanton woman inside me had come unleashed at Stone's touch. I didn't know her and she frightened me. But she knew what she wanted. The eagerness to hold nothing back and take it all. Everything I knew Stone would give me I became desperate for. I didn't understand my reaction. I knew the hedonism Stone could provide was what I desired above all else.

The darkness swirling in his eyes should have made me nervous but all I could do was beg for more. There was no limit as long as Stone was touching me. His hand slid up my thigh and with one finger he began to open me with a roughness that excited me. I wanted it to hurt a little. I wanted him to lay his claim on me, leaving me aching.

"It's tight," he said as his gaze was on the area opened to him. "My dick is going to split you open."

"Yes," the sound of that made me squirm with restless

anticipation. This was like a tease that kept me at the verge of an orgasm and dangled me there. I wanted to be tossed over the edge, but then jerked back and tossed again and again.

His pupils completely dominated the color of his eyes. Stone's mouth opened slightly as he lifted his body from mine and removed his clothing with quick determination. I was lost the moment I got the full view of his body. Beautiful and more perfect than I'd realized. Every inch of him was cut as if he were a god. I was anxious to touch him.

When his body covered mine, the power emanating from him had be lifting myself to get there sooner. I was impatient. He used one hand to hold me back and I almost pleaded with him to let me touch him as he stripped my tank top off my body. I'd forgotten I was still wearing it. My focus had been on him.

When I was bared to him completely, I paused. I was unsure for the first time since he kissed me. His body was perfectly chiseled. It was intimidating.

His eyes roamed over me and all I could see now were the girls. The topless ones, naked ones, and beautiful bodies he'd been with at the Van Allan pool parties.

I closed my eyes wishing I hadn't remembered them, the parties, or the girls. When Jasper had seen me like this I hadn't felt so self-conscious. But now, with Stone, I worried I wouldn't meet his expectations.

"Open your eyes, Beulah." It wasn't a gentle request. His words were an order and I obeyed. My willing obedience was unlike me, but Stone made me react in a way no one ever had. There was some unseen power there that ignited when we were near each other. Even when I thought I hated him, I found myself looking for him. As if my soul was attached to his even though neither of us seemed to want that.

"Open your legs wider," he said his voice hoarse. If I didn't know better, I could've sworn he was trembling. Was his control slipping? Did he feel this unknown energy between us too?

His nostrils flared as I felt his hardness brush against my sensitive core. "I wanted to make love to you. Kiss you, get so damn much of you on my skin that I could smell it for days. But now." He growled as his eyes glowed. "I need to fuck you. Hard. Take it all. Here you scream my name."

It was me who trembled now. I shook and wanted to beg him for exactly that. What he was explaining was unknown to me. A dark, exciting temptation I wanted with him. There was no fear. I trusted him.

Lifting my hips, I felt him press closer to the entrance causing more sizzling pressure. It was beginning to be too much. I felt as if I might explode any moment. The knowledge that he was going to fill me was sending bolts of electricity throughout my entire body.

"Mine," he said loudly in a harsh tone.

My breath left me as my body rocketed and I was full. Beautifully invaded. Stretched and crying out in pleasure while I clung to him. He was too big. Yet the sharp pain was everything and more. I cried his name and begged him for more.

"Fucking mine," he repeated and began moving. In and out. Each rock of his hips brought me closer to the beauty that I knew only he could give me. Nothing before this mattered. Nothing after this would ever measure up. This was a pinnacle that I never knew existed.

"Stone," I breathed. "I need," I couldn't string the words together. He was inside me bringing me to the edge that I wanted to leap off and fall into it blindly. Not caring about anything but this. Us.

"You need this?" he asked as he began pumping into me harder. His mouth lowered and devoured one of my nipples. Biting. Creating new currents that made me shake.

His mouth moved up my chest and licked at my collarbone. He took bites of my skin as he worked his way up my neck. When his warm breath caressed my ear, I clung to him tighter. I was about to erupt. Each brush of his mouth against my skin and every jerk of his hips had my knees lifting higher. My ankles crossed over his back trying to get him deeper.

Stone bit my earlobe and whispered, "I want to come inside you. Fill you until it's running down your sweet thighs. All I can think about is how fucking amazing it would be to be inside you while I explode."

All of that. I wanted it. "Yes. Please," I sounded desperate. Like a woman in a desert that sees water. It was all I needed. My nails clawed at his back.

"Fuck," he said as he got rougher. My hips slamming into the bed. "You make me insane," he growled. "Fucking crazed."

"Oh God! Please!" I threw my head back. It was there. I was falling. The world was gone from underneath me. Nothing around me existed. It was a divine experience. "STONE!" I heard my voice cry out for him. I could hear him talking, but the other world I was floating in muffled it all.

"FUUUUCK!" his roar brought me back enough to witness him pull out of me to watch his release shoot all over my stomach. The sight of it excited me. Made me forget I'd just been given the most life altering experience of my life and I already wanted more.

His eyes lifted from the view of my stomach to meet my

dazed eyes. He was panting. Trying to catch his breath. Sweat clung to his skin. His eyes had more color than black now. "Holy hell," he whispered.

I touched the hot seed on my stomach. Curious about how it felt and liking the image of it on my fingers.

"Jesus Christ, Beulah," he said with a small laugh. "I'm going to toss you over and fuck you again, this time so I can worship that ass of yours if you don't stop. I'll never get enough of you. Of this."

A slow smile spread across my face as I lifted my fingers and tasted his release. I felt wanton and I loved it.

His eyes flared again and I knew our night wasn't over.

Chapter Twenty-Four
STONE

ACKNOWLEDGING MY RELATIONSHIP with Jasper wasn't more important than Beulah hadn't been a quick thing. I'd battled it. Fought it. But in the end, there was only so much room in my heart and Beulah was quickly filling it. The more I got to know her, the further I was consumed.

Last night had been it. Changed it all. Every step, every choice, all of it from now on would be centered around Beulah. She had slowly become my life. I didn't regret it. How could I when I had never felt such complete joy in my entire life? Any darkness, pain, anger that had been a constant in my life didn't matter. She drowned it all out just by being near me.

I would fight. I would face whatever necessary to keep her.

Taking a drink of my coffee I continued to lean against the doorframe watching her sleep. We'd had another intense round last night where I was positive I left a hand print on her left butt cheek. I woke her up after a few hours' sleep and made love to her. We took it slow that time. I tasted her while she squirmed and pulled my hair.

The memory made me hard. I had to keep my distance as she slept now.

She needed her rest. Even in her sleep there she smiled softly. I'd put that there. My chest felt like it would explode. The idea of beating my hands against it like a cave man was tempting. She was asleep and completed exhausted because I'd given her more pleasure than she could take. I wasn't an easy man to love. I was easier to hate. I knew that.

But if I could keep her by giving her that kind of pleasure, I saw that as a win-win for both of us. Being inside her was more than just a fuck. It was more than an erotic experience. It was mind blowing. Soul claiming.

She stretched causing her small feet to peek out from the covers. Her arms lifted over her head and she yawned. I enjoyed witnessing such pure beauty. If I hadn't spent most of the night naked and inside her I'd say it was the picture of innocence. Even though I'd had her clinging to me, clawing me, and begging me to fuck her, she still held that beautiful innocent glow.

Blonde hair spread out over the pillow as she turned her head toward me. Two slow blinks and then a small shy smile. Exactly as I'd imagined it. I'd watched her, studied her, and been fascinated by her from day one. I knew her expressions. I knew what made her smile and how to cause anger to flash in her stunning eyes. When she tried to hide an emotion, I knew it. There was little I didn't know.

"Hi," she whispered then turned to face me.

"Hi," I replied. I stayed where I was enjoying the view. Trying like hell to believe it was real and not some fleeting dream.

She sat up taking the covers with her to keep her naked body covered—as if I hadn't memorized every inch of it already. But the modesty was cute. It was Beulah. I wouldn't want her to change anything. She was exactly what I wanted.

"Have you been up long?" she asked sitting there with her legs tucked underneath her.

"Not too long. I didn't want to disturb you, so I made coffee and decided that watching you from a safe distance was better."

She ducked her head and blushed. The shyness after last night's wild and wicked events was as adorable as it was silly. She'd begged me to fuck her just hours ago. Now she was red in the face knowing I watched her sleep.

"I've licked your slick pussy, bit your ass, and shot my come all over your stomach, back, and tits. Yet my watching you sleep embarrasses you?" I was teasing her. Taunting even.

She lifted her head and the twinkle of mischief in her eyes made it hard to continue standing where I was. I wanted to be there in bed with her. Doing it all again.

Gripping the covers against her she jumped up frantically. "Oh my God! Geraldine!"

I'd almost forgotten about that. "I called her yesterday when I was headed back home. Let her know that you would need today off. I arranged for a friend of hers to take her shopping today. She's excited about it."

The small crease between her eyebrows as she measured my words was cute. I gave her time to process. She needed to know that last night wasn't a spontaneous reckless decision for me. I'd wanted it. Hoped for it.

"You knew we would . . . do this?" She was still frowning. I didn't want her to think I'd taken her for granted. I hadn't.

"No. What happened last night was so much more than I hoped for. But I did want time with you. Time to show you exactly how I felt. Time to find out if there was a chance. If this could happen."

Her tense expression eased and the frown faded. A soft smile curled along her swollen pink lips. I would never lie to her. She'd had too many lies in her life so far. The truth, however, was a gamble. She may not always like to hear it. That wasn't important now.

"Are you sore?" I asked her before she could say anything.

She paused then gave a small shrug. "No. Not really."

That had been the answer I wanted to hear. However, I'd make sure the next time I asked she said yes. Sitting my coffee cup down on the table beside the door I went to her taking long strides. Her eyes went wide and excitement sparked in them.

"Drop the covers, Beulah," I demanded and loved that she did just that. Exposing her naked breasts that were firm and high. Hard nipples showed her arousal. She tilted her head up to watch me. There was a bite mark on her neck and I felt a greedy, possessive smirk break out on my face. I'd done that.

"Turn around. Put your hands on the bed. Stick your hot little ass up in the air."

Her breathing was now rapid as she listened to my directions. She didn't question me. She moved slowly as her eyes stayed locked with mine. As she stood, the covers dropped, baring her to me completely. Then she did exactly as I had instructed.

There was a slight pink mark on her left cheek. I touched it, gently outlining it with the tip of my finger. Then I ran my thumb over it to soothe it before sliding my hand between her legs to shove them open wider. Then I pressed down on her back with my palm. "I want it higher," I said as her ass lifted toward me.

My dick throbbed. The blood swelled in the head as I watched her prepare for me. For it. I feared I'd never let her out of this apartment again. I had images of her naked spread out on my bar in the kitchen. Of her standing under the water in the shower as I knelt on my knees between her legs. Of her hands against the glass of my patio doors looking outside at the world around us as I sank into her from behind. The thrill of someone seeing us and the possessive fear of anyone else seeing her like this fought against me.

I slipped a finger inside her and she jerked. "You said you weren't sore," I said gently testing her.

"That's not pain, it's need," she was panting as she spoke.

I used one hand to shove my boxers down, kicking them aside. Closing one hand over my cock, I pumped it while I touched her. The wetness pooling between her legs coating my fingers the way it soon would my dick. It jerked in my hand wanting what I was in my blatant view. The unparalleled pleasure she gave me was turning me into an addict. Her tight pussy was my drug.

Unable to tease either of us anymore, I grabbed her waist and jerked her ass up even higher. Her legs spread open as she went up on her toes. I used no restraint as I pushed into her tight entrance. Her slick hole sucked me in and squeezed.

"OH GOD!" she screamed.

I wasn't sure there was a God, but when her pussy massaged my dick like a vice I was pretty damn sure that only a greater being could create something this beautiful.

"Feel good, baby? Is that what you want? A hard morning fuck," my voice was laced with the tension of my building release. Deep and hoarse.

"Yes! Harder. Fuck me until I can't stand up," she begged then turned her head to look back at me. Her hands gripping the covers and fisting them. "I want you to come on my face."

"Shit!" I roared. Hearing talk like that from her sweet mouth was going to cause me to blow before I was ready. "Keep talking like that and I'm going to lose my load before I can get out of you. Your pussy is an addiction."

She gave me a wicked grin and I pounded her so hard I was afraid it was too much. Her eyes closed and she moaned. I did it again and she threw her head back and moaned louder. Reaching up, I grabbed a handful of hair and pulled it back.

"AH! YES!" she cried.

This little perfect beauty was naughty as hell. I hadn't realized that until last night. That knowledge made me feel animalistic when I was inside her. I wanted to do things to her I should be fucking ashamed of.

"Take it," I said and kept up the hard rhythm. My dick was so damn swollen I knew my release was close. But I couldn't pull out. Stopping was impossible. Not when her imminent pulsing release felt like a silken vice around me.

"Oh God! There! Oh GOD! I'm," she cried. "Please. HARD!" Her ass raised higher and she pushed back against me. "I can't stop!" she was panicked and fucking me back. Her ass slapping my thighs. "Yes, yes, yes," the panting was her orgasm. I couldn't pull out until she was done but her orgasm continued. Her body was wild against mine. She tightened on my dick and I began shaking as I tried to keep from losing it.

"Oh God, again! It's coming again," she shook and trembled and her ass bounced against me, the soft skin jiggling from the wild movements. Her cries of pleasure grew. I was there and nothing on earth could stop me. My hands clasped her waist so hard I knew she'd have marks.

"BEULAH!" I roared as I spilled into her. My release pumped relentlessly as she kept slapping against me panting.

"UUUUUHHHHH!!!! A. . A . . . AGAIN," she said as she stilled with her ass pressed tightly against me. Her body was shaking violently. My seed was so deep inside her, marking her. The beauty of the moment was more than I could have imagined.

Her head collapsed on the bed and she let out a long sigh. "Sweet Jesus," her voice was hoarse now.

I eased my grip on her hips. Then picked her up and moved her until she was lying on the bed. I'd never gone without protection with a woman. Ever. It was something I prided myself on. I had a case of condoms in my bedroom. But not once had I considered using them with her. Not last night. Not this morning. And not when I was pouring into her. I couldn't even muster regret.

Instead, I opened her legs and she blinked. She gazed up at me before she willingly let her legs fall open. The inner beast inside me touched her with one finger and I fucking memorized the way my semen looked leaking from her. Wet on her thighs. That was me on her skin.

"I should apologize. But I can't," I told her honestly.

"I'd be disappointed if you did."

Unable to take my eyes from the proof of our pleasure, I ran a finger over the wetness now trickling down to her bottom. She shivered. "Ah."

"I'll be more careful from now on. I swear," I told her.

She leaned up on her elbows. Her breasts now catching my attention. "I'd rather get on birth control. I like the way this feels. Just feeling the warmth inside me made my orgasm so intense. I want that again."

"Fuck," I whispered. "Yeah, well, you need to get on that ASAP. All I want to do is sink inside you, Beulah. It's starting to scare the hell out of me."

She sat up, her legs still open to me. "You make me want to do things," she paused and smiled. "Bad things. Good things. All of it."

I closed her legs then. If I didn't, I'd end up between them again. And I didn't care what she said. After that last bout, she had to be bruised. Reaching for her, I pulled her into my lap, kissed her temple, then held her against me.

"Today, let's stay here. In this apartment. Alone," I suggested.

She snuggled against me. "Okay. Are we going to have more sex?" The hopeful sound in her voice made me chuckle.

"I tell you what. We'll go eat breakfast. After, we'll take a shower and I'll kiss between your legs until you come on my face. I don't care what you say, you've got to be sore now."

She ran a hand up my chest. "Oh, I'm sore. Raw even. Maybe a little bruised. But the idea of you doing it again while I'm so tender, making my eyes water from the pain, it seems erotic."

I closed my eyes and inhaled as my fucking dick twitched back to life under her bottom.

"Beulah. We're going to fuck each other to death."

She kissed my chin and replied, "You say that like it's a bad thing."

Chapter Twenty-Five
BEULAH

THE SMELL OF bread filled the kitchen as I opened the oven to take out the loaf I'd made to go with our simple fettuccini alfredo dinner. Other than eggs and fruit for breakfast, a shared sub sandwich for lunch that he'd fed me part of, we'd eaten nothing else.

I had learned today that sexual activity was as exhausting as it was pleasurable. My body felt as if I'd just ran a marathon and it still hummed from our activities. I knew if he came in here and pulled up the T-shirt I was wearing I'd gladly bend over and let him have me again. He kept saying he was addicted to me but I feared it was the other way around.

While he was returning a work phone call as I finished my dinner, I couldn't stop thinking about how his mouth had felt between my legs. The way his tongue had sucked and flicked my clit until I'd gone wild. It tingled as I thought about it. I was excited again and could feel my inner thighs dampening. I'd decided panties were pointless and all I was wearing was one of Stone's T-shirts.

Slicing the bread, I wondered if something was wrong with me. Was it normal for a woman to be so sex crazed? I hadn't been this way with Jasper. It had been sweet and I had enjoyed it but . . . our lovemaking was never like this. When Stone touched me, I felt like an open electric socket. Everything was so powerful and some dark part of me desired things I never thought I'd want.

Did Stone bring this out in all women? Was his talent at sex what was causing this? Had that been why Presley was so insane when it came to him? That thought put a damper on my mood.

I'd been so wrapped up in it all that I had forgotten he'd been with a lot of women. I was one in a long line. He was definitely the best I'd ever had but I had very limited experience. Although I knew what was happening with him was rare. It was rare for me. Maybe it was normal for him.

I stopped slicing the bread and looked at the wall across from me. I sighed as my mood plummeted. Was I so naïve that I had missed all that? Was my craving for how he made me feel hindering common sense? Reality?

He hadn't said he loved me. Not really. He said "he knew he would love me." At that instant, I knew I was in love with him. Everything clicked into place. It all made perfect sense. My denial vanished and I accepted the truth. I let go of my guilt and embraced loving Stone. But he had never said that he loved me.

I had cried out that I loved him more than once right before my world was lit up again and again and I spiraled into bliss. But he'd never repeated it back.

"Smells good," his voice broke into my thoughts and I turned my head to look at him. I wanted to see if the unspoken words were there in his eyes. Something to reassure me I wasn't being careless with my heart. I'd let him come inside me. I had even reveled in how it felt to be filled with his seed. But now . . . had I been impulsive, reckless?

"What's wrong?" his concern was immediate and he took long, quick strides until he was beside me. He turned me around to face him. His hands caged me in against the counter, and his eyes that I'd once thought were cold and void of emotion showed so much. "You're upset. Why?"

I could hide the truth, but lies and hiding had already hurt too many people in my life. I wasn't going to add to it. "I was just . . . I was thinking about us. How it feels. How . . . how it's unlike anything I've known. It seems unreal. Like a fantasy. But I-I don't have much experience. This may be normal . . . for you."

I wanted to ask him if he loved me. But the words wouldn't come out.

He lifted one eyebrow. "Normal?" he repeated as if he couldn't believe I'd asked that. I simply nodded.

A naughty smirk lifted the corner of his lips. "I told you I was addicted to you. I can't leave this apartment because if I'm not inside you my damn dick is hard and waiting until it can be again. Nothing about this is normal. It's the most magnificent, spectacular experience of my life." I could see the teasing gleam in his eyes. He meant what he was saying but he was also teasing me for asking.

"Do you love me?" I blurted out the words. I had to ask him. Even if the answer was no, I had to know.

He studied me a moment. Then he pressed his body closer and cupped my left cheek in his hand. He bent down and pressed a kiss to my mouth. "You own my heart. Love seems too weak a word for this Beulah. But if that's what you need to hear. Yes,

I love you."

Love wasn't a weak word. It was powerful. It was the most important thing a human being could experience. Love was precious and unique. And once you experienced it, you were changed. There were different levels of love. There were loves you'd never lose. There were loves that came for a time and marked you. There were loves that were beautiful and fleeting. But each one was important. Each one the grandest part of life.

He ran a hand through my hair. Letting his fingers tangle in the locks. I leaned into his touch. "Loving someone is as close to heaven we can experience on earth," I told him.

He gave me a crooked grin. "No, Beulah. When I'm deep inside you is as close to heaven on earth as it'll ever get. Hell, baby, I'd argue that even heaven isn't that sacred."

I slapped his arm. "Stone, don't say that."

He leaned down and kissed me. Long and slow. Sweet and soft. I wrapped my arms around his neck and enjoyed the taste and emotion that came from the connection. His hands ran down my body, cupped my bottom and picked me up. I wrapped my legs around his waist as he walked me over to the table.

"How much longer does the pasta have?" he asked.

"Twenty minutes," I told him. "Longer if I put it to simmer."

"Twenty minutes is good," he said. His pants were already pulled down and he was inside me. Slowly he sank in, and I winced but it was a delicious feeling. "I swore I was going to give you time before I was inside you again but I can't. I want to stay up inside you. No end."

"Me too," I agreed. "I love being sore from you," I told him. "It excites me. I feel naughty having been used so much it hurts."

He growled and his jaw clenched. "I'm going slow this time.

Stop taunting me. You make me lose it and it hurts you. If you'll keep that naughty little mouth shut we will do this slow and easy."

I ran my hands over my breasts as he watched me, sliding my right hand down to touch where he entered me. He froze and watched as I began playing with my swollen clit. When he started moving again he was breathing hard and his eyes were on me touching myself.

The excitement in his gaze only added to the way it made me feel. I was showing him how I pleased myself while he pleased me even more.

"Do you touch yourself when you're alone?" he asked huskily.

"Yes. When I'm in the bath," I admitted.

"I want to fuck you hard. Watch you scream. Watch you come apart under me. Keep touching that pussy and I will. My restraint is almost gone, baby."

I lifted my hand away and his eyes followed my finger as I moved it to my mouth and licked it.

"Jesus," he muttered.

I stuck my tongue out and ran the finger over it to the tip then used the finger to begin to play again. That was his breaking point. He grabbed my thighs and rocked deep into me with no restraint. When I moaned his name, he moved faster. His eyes glazed over from the building release we both knew was coming.

I held my knees up to his waist and he grabbed my left one and pulled my ankle up to his shoulder. He was deeper now. I sucked in air at the shock.

"Do you think about this when you play with that pussy?" he asked.

"Yes!" I admitted. I had thought of him many times even when I felt guilty for it.

"You're gonna play with it tonight. I'm going to stand over you and watch until I shoot my load all over your hand and thighs."

The idea of that made my body hum with more wicked heat. "AH! AH!" I was so close. "Stone! Yes! Oh, oh!" The light shattered around me. I grabbed at his arms and felt my nails sink into his skin.

"GOD! FUCK! I CAN'T," he yelled and the heat from his release was shot inside me as his body shook. "HELL!"

The heat and simple knowledge he was coming inside me was intense. His release of pleasure in my body sent me spiraling further into that world of ecstasy. The one I wanted to live in.

Stone lowered his body over mine and his face buried in my neck. "Jesus, Beulah. I can't do that again. But you make it so hard to pull away. I want to be inside you when I come. That is love, baby. Pure fucking love."

I giggled and pressed my lips to his head. "When you let me leave this apartment again I will get birth control. It takes 30 days before it works though."

He lifted slightly. "There's a shot that works immediately. You need that. You'll be pregnant in a month."

Although he was teasing he was also serious.

"Okay. I'll get the shot."

He sighed. "Thank you."

"I should check on the pasta," I reminded him.

"Sorry I forgot," he said moving off me. "Need me to get you a towel for between your legs?"

I stood up letting the T-shirt slide back over me. "No. I like how it feels." I walked past him and went to check the fettuccini. After taking it off the stove and stirring it I looked up to find him watching me.

"It's ready."

"I won't be able to eat thinking about my come dripping down your thighs."

"Why not?"

He ran a hand through his hair and groaned. "You are going to kill me."

Laughing, I grabbed plates from the cabinets and wondered if I should fear the future. Could I face losing him? Or should I enjoy the present and forget about the pain I might face one day.

"Beulah," he said my name and I turned to him.

"You, are my fate."

I stood there a moment and let that sink in. Then I realized I was wrong. Maybe there was something stronger than love.

Chapter Twenty-Six
STONE

I WATCHED HER car drive away from the window of my apartment. When I'd woken up in the middle of the night with an ache for her I'd fought it off. She needed her rest. Keeping her home with me locked away from the world two days in a row was selfish. I had to find a way to go through the day without having her right there beside me. This was new for me, the constant yearning.

Gerry would fill her ears full of stories from her day out shopping before she forgot what year it was and began planning some event or a visit where dead people would be involved. Seeing her with Gerry had been the last straw for me. Fighting this thing that pulled me to her had been hard enough. Reminding myself that Jasper loved her and although I knew he'd never be able to be the man she deserved, I tried to be a good man. The kind that didn't go after the woman his best friend loved.

Eventually, that didn't matter. When your fate is made clear, you can't run from it. It owns you. And you want it to. You fucking thank God for it.

Once her car was completely out of sight, I sighed and stepped away from the window. I had to get my head clear enough to focus on work. I also needed to plan how to deal with Jasper. This wasn't something he needed to find out through our social network. Because I didn't plan on hiding this. Beulah would be with me publically. I had a charity event that my father expected me to attend here in Savannah next weekend. Beulah would go with me. Jasper would know within hours. That is if he didn't come himself.

I walked back to the kitchen and cleaned the cup I'd used for my coffee. I loaded the dishwasher with my cup and Beulah's. Her scent was all over the place. As much as I loved it, the sweet lingering fragrance made it hard to think of anything else. She had work. I should work. Tonight, however, I'd take her on the balcony. Late. In the darkness. Covering her mouth so no one could hear her cries of pleasure.

Fuck, now I needed a cold shower. It was like I was fifteen again and the house cleaner my dad had hired was bouncing around in low cut tops and no bra in front of me daily. She had kept me in a constant state of arousal. I'd masturbated to the image of her tits for weeks, until she walked in and caught me. She went down on her knees and sucked me off that day. Shaking my head, I shoved that memory away. Hilda had become one of my stepmothers a few months later. Just more of my twisted childhood.

I was walking out of the kitchen when the front door swung open. "STONE!" Presley's voice echoed through the apartment. Nothing could have gotten rid of my hard on any faster. Motherfucker, I wasn't in the mood for this.

Rounding the corner, I found her there with black streaks of mascara running down her face as she sobbed dramatically. This was an act. I knew it just like I'd always known her fake displays of emotion. I watched her as she put her show into motion.

"He took my money. Stole from me! Then left!" she wailed.

I wasn't surprised. The man was a con artist. I had tried to tell her that when she moved in with me the last time he had abandoned her. This time I wasn't wasting my breath.

"Why are you barging into my home unannounced? I wasn't aware I needed to change the locks. There's a doorbell. Use it." My tone was cold. Flat. Bored.

She paused a moment. Not prepared for that response. She had hoped for concern. Sympathy. And I wasn't reacting the way she wanted. Her routine would need a last-minute adjustment. I could see it in her eyes as she quickly changed her course. "I know you warned me but I was hurt, Stone. You had that woman here. You know how I feel about you. And she was thrown in my face, where I lived. It hurt me. I wanted to feel loved and Wesley made me feel that way."

They were a good pair. Presley and Wesley. They both used others for their benefit until they were finished with them. I had no time for this. I was used to being alone here. Now, this was Beulah's home too. I wanted my life with her to be just that. With her. Presley couldn't be a part of that. She wouldn't want to.

"You're grown. You have a job and can get a place of your own. You're living here was temporary. Things have changed. It's no longer an option for you to live here."

I pulled my phone out of my pocket and checked the time. "It's almost eight and I need to get dressed for work. The next time you decide to enter my home without an invitation I will call the police."

I didn't give her time to react. To get angry. I walked past her. Opened the front door and held it open. "Goodbye, Presley."

She didn't move. Her eyes narrowed and she glared at me. When she didn't get her way she often acted like an irate five-year-old. "You're tossing me out?" her voice was incredulous.

"You left already. I never had to toss you."

"You pushed me away. Over and over. I love you, but you won't see that. You don't care. You can't love." Her anger eased some. She was changing course. "We were good, Stone. You fucked me like I have never been fucked," she dropped her voice to what she thought was a sexy tone. "I loved having your dick shoved down my throat. Making me gag. Pushing too far. Having your hot come on my tongue. I still taste it. Want it. I'm thirsty for it." She was now closing in on me. As her hands reached to touch me, I grabbed them both and moved her back.

"Don't touch me. It's time for you to go."

She wasn't going to be easily convinced. "Don't you want it? My mouth sucking hard on your dick. Like a lollipop on my lips. My fingers inside me pleasuring myself as I take all of you as far down my throat as I can—"

"You're wasting my time. The answer is no. I don't want my dick near any part of you. I'm sure there are thousands of men who do. Go find one."

Fury was there in her eyes and I knew she was about to snap. At least we had come to the end of this ridiculous visit.

"It's her, isn't it? She's still here! You're fucking her! She's white trash, Stone! Low class—"

I reached for her and grabbing her arm I physically moved her out of my apartment. This was for her safety. Hearing her speak about Beulah like that was pushing me to a place she'd never seen me and didn't want to experience.

"Leave," I commanded.

"Is it that good?" she spat at me. "It'll get old. Her trashy roots can't keep you happy. You like expensive things, Stone."

"I'm closing this door and giving you three minutes to exit this building before I call the police to escort you out. Do I make myself clear?"

She threw her shoulders back like I had insulted her. Like she hadn't entered my home without an invitation. I didn't wait for her to open her mouth and say anything more.

The slam of the door was a relief. It was the end to that part of my life. The end to fixing my dad's loose ends. His world was not mine.

Chapter Twenty-Seven
BEULAH

AFTER CLOSING GERALDINE'S bedroom door quietly, I left her there to nap. We had worked out in her garden today. Part of the time, she'd been here in the present. The other part it had been 1953. She was tired from her outing yesterday and asked me to help her reorganize her closet. However, when we had gotten up there she'd decided she needed rest. Five minutes later, she was softly snoring.

There were dishes in the dishwasher I needed to unload and dusting in the parlor I was going to get to today. It had been hard not to think about Stone all day. His smile, his scowl, his voice when he was inside me. Shivering at the thought, I went to the kitchen and stood there a moment. Remembering how he'd bathed me last night. Then how we had made love gently at first as the water hit us from above. So quickly it had turned naughty. Wild. With my entire front pressed against the marble wall of the shower while he entered me, his body covering mine. Every time he slammed into me, my feet lifted from the floor. He'd growled in my ear with every thrust.

Before I could reach my climax, he would pull back. Bringing me there time and again, then letting it fade slightly. I'd been so desperate that I began pleading for him to make me come.

He pulled my hair and bit my ear roughly. It was his words that had sent me crying and almost collapsing from the orgasm that hit me. "Next time I'm going to shove this dick in your pretty mouth and watch your eyes water as you gag. I want to see my come running down your neck. Coating you."

All I had been able to think about since I woke up this morning was my mouth on him. I'd wanted to try it this morning, but I couldn't be late. Instead, I had fantasized about it whenever I got a chance.

Walking over to the pantry, my thoughts were on my mouth doing things to Stone. The hand that reached out and grabbed my wrist when I opened the door startled me, and before I could scream a hand covered my mouth. I was pulled into the dark pantry. My mind was trying to figure out what was happening and what to do. I couldn't let whoever this was find Geraldine.

"It's me," Stone said in my ear. He removed his hand and I let out a relieved breath before spinning around to face him.

"What in the world are you doing? Trying to scare me to death?" I asked unable to see his face clearly in the darkness. The light seeping from under the pantry door gave us enough illumination that I could make out his body in front of me.

"I need to fuck you," he said as he jerked my shorts down.

"You snuck in to abduct me in the pantry and have sex with me?" I asked my heart now racing for other reasons.

"Yes," he growled. "All I can think about is being inside you.

I can't get shit done."

"Geraldine could come down here and hear us," I reminded him.

"Not if you're a good girl and don't make any noise."

I wasn't sure that was possible. "Stone! We can't do this," I argued, but it was feeble. The idea of him taking me in the pantry with Geraldine upstairs was exciting.

"Take your shorts off, Beulah," he demanded.

I did. I pushed them all the way down and kicked the discarded clothing aside. I knew we could get caught. I didn't want Geraldine to catch us. But I'd been in a constant state of arousal thinking about Stone's hardness in my mouth. Choking me. He picked me up and pressed my back against the wall. He kissed my neck as he slid into me in one swift push taking my breath away.

I wrapped my legs around him to hold on as he rocked into me over and over. "Such a dirty girl," he said as he nuzzled my neck. "Pulling your pants off and giving me this pussy in a pantry."

I whimpered. The naughtiness of the situation and his hard body taking me like this was almost more than I could handle. I wanted to cry out. Beg for more. But I bit my bottom lip and held it in.

"That's it. Be nice and quiet while I fuck this pussy. All I could think about. Can't function from needing this. The thought of you makes me so damn hard."

I buried my face in his chest to muffle the noises I was making.

"You're soaking wet, Beulah. Was the fear of someone taking you exciting enough to arouse you?"

I shook my head. "I've been thinking about sucking you all day. What you said last night," I whispered, the darkness making me bold.

Air hissed between his teeth. "Thinking about taking my dick in your mouth made you wet?"

"Yes," I admitted with a sigh of pleasure.

He began moving faster. His pants were hard and right at my ear. "Fuck, fuck, fuck," his chant made my climax climb faster. The beating of his heart matched my own.

"That's it, take it like the dirty girl you are," he whispered as his body began to grow taunt.

The peak washed over me. I started to cry out and his hand covered my mouth. His eyes locked with mine as I shattered to pieces in his arms. Then he pulled from me. "I'm coming," he growled and groaned as he pumped his release all over my thighs as I watched with fascination.

We were both panting as we stood there in the darkness. I wished I had been able to see clearer. My eyes had adjusted to the darkness, but I had wanted to see his eyes when he had pulled away and he reached his own pleasure.

"I'll clean you up," he said softly.

I watched as he found a paper towel roll in the corner and began to wipe himself from my skin. Once he finished he lifted his eyes to meet mine. "Tonight, you're taking me in your mouth. I doubt I can focus on much else now. But that will help get me through."

I started to get my shorts and he stopped me. "I'll do that."

I stood there as he dressed me. My heart full. My body sated.

Footsteps stopped us both. A grin that I could see in the darkness curled on his lips. "Better get out there. She'll be looking for you."

I quickly straightened my hair and opened the door to step out, hoping she didn't notice I was walking out of a dark pantry with nothing.

Geraldine was at the sink. "I think we should have tea out on the veranda," she said cheerfully.

"Okay, yes, that's a good idea. I have the tea cakes and sandwiches you mentioned earlier in the fridge." I sounded nervous. She didn't seem to notice.

"Lovely. It's perfect weather for tea outside." She took the tray with the teapot. "You get the nibbles and I'll take this."

"Okay," I readily agreed.

I quickly found the items I had made earlier today when she'd mentioned she'd like to have them. But not before I took a quick glance at the pantry. Having our tea outside would give Stone time to leave without being seen.

Geraldine opened the door to the backyard and paused. "Oh, and Beulah," she said.

"Yes?"

"Grab another cup and tell Stone that I'd love for him to get out of my pantry to join us for tea."

Chapter Twenty-Eight
STONE

MACK WAS STANDING outside the apartment building with a cigarette in his mouth when I pulled into the parking lot just before seven. I wanted to be home when Beulah arrived. She'd been a nervous mess during tea with Gerry today. Although Gerry had only mentioned she knew we'd fucked in her pantry once. It had been a side note at that. She hadn't seemed to be surprised or upset about it. That didn't matter to Beulah. She was so fidgety and couldn't hide her expressive eyes. It was damn cute.

Getting out of my Range Rover, I pocketed my keys and phone and headed toward Mack. He had a purpose for being out here other than to smoke. His apartment had the same balcony mine had. If he'd wanted a smoke he could have used his. His presence when he expected me home meant something.

"What do you need?" I asked bluntly. I didn't have time for beating around the bush with small talk.

Mack took a long drag from his Marlboro and let the smoke that didn't damage his lungs back out of his nose and mouth. "You dating Beulah?"

I'd known this was about her. When I had gone to his apartment to get her, I knew then she was in his sights. The man had no morals. I'd been furious and ready to kick him out when I'd found her there. It had taken extreme self-control not to lose my shit.

"It's more than dating. But if you're asking if she's available, then no she isn't. And she won't be. Ever."

Beulah was a beautiful woman. Men wanted her. I understood that. But dealing with it head on was difficult. My possessive nature flared and I wanted to act like a fucking maniac to get my point across. I refrained. Barely.

"I thought it was headed that way. Wasn't sure. Wanted to check first."

I waited for him to say more. When he didn't, I walked past him and focused on getting inside before I planted my fist in his face for nothing. My temper needed checking.

"She's different. She wasn't like the others. I didn't want her the way you think I did. I was interested in more," Mack added just before I escaped him.

That admission should make me feel better. It didn't. He wanted what I had. He wanted what I already knew. She was a rare find. I took a deep breath and forced myself to admit that this was unavoidable. She was special. Other men would see it. I had to learn to live with that.

"She's mine." The simple statement sounded chauvinistic even for my own ears. At that moment, I didn't give a fuck. It was the truth. I was big on brutal honesty. Why hold back now?

He gave a nod. "Not planning on making a move. I had a

feeling. Like I said. Just wanted to make sure I wasn't getting the wrong signals."

"You weren't," I barked more than replied and went inside before he could say more. I was almost to my floor when I realized he was still out there. She'd be home soon. Knowing how he felt, I didn't want him waiting on her if that was what he was doing. Pausing, I started to turn around when the door opened and I heard Shay say, "I got the damn pie. Jesus stop bitching."

"It's about time you did something right," Mack replied.

"When I had your dick down my throat and you were shouting for me to swallow it all I didn't hear any complaints," Shay shot back at him.

"Baby, you want me putting you on your knees and doing it again then keep talking. I have thought of little else since you took my entire load then licked those fat lips of yours."

It was quiet then. I didn't move simply because I didn't want them to know I'd heard this interaction. It wasn't my business. Although the reminder that Beulah wanted my dick in her mouth had me hardening as they discussed it.

"Maybe that's exactly what I want," Shay replied.

"Marty won't be here for another thirty minutes. Get your hot little ass inside and get on your knees."

"Will you shoot it on my face this time?"

"Hell yes, I will," he replied.

The door opened and closed quickly behind them. Turning, I went into my apartment fully erect. Knowing that Shay was taking Mack right now the way I wanted Beulah to take me was fucking with my head. It hadn't been my conversation to overhear, but I'd heard it nonetheless.

I turned on lights as I went through the house and waited

impatiently for Beulah to get home. I knew she cooked dinner for Gerry and they ate together. I loved that she did it. But right now, I needed her more than Gerry did.

I began pacing the living room when the door finally opened.

I walked to the entrance to see her standing there. Her cheeks pink with anticipation. She was thinking about it. I wasn't the only one aroused. Her eyes said enough.

I began unzipping my jeans, my willpower long gone. I didn't even have to say anything. She was in front of me slowly lowering herself to her knees. No words. Nothing. Just the excited gleam in her eyes. My cock throbbed and I felt pure adoration for the woman now kneeling in front of me.

She touched the sensitive swollen head then lifted her eyes back to meet mine. "Tell me what to do," she said. "I want to do it right."

She could lick it like a damn lollipop and I'd explode. I was that far gone. Having her mouth that close to my arousal was enough for me. But she was sincere. She wanted to know.

"Slid it into your mouth. Suck on it like you would a lollipop. Run your tongue over it. Take it as deep as you can."

She studied the throbbing monster in her hand then did exactly as I said. I watched as my knees began to buckle at the sight. Her mouth was like a fucking vacuum as she sucked hard. The moan of pleasure that came from her vibrated through my dick and sent a thrill through the rest of my body.

"That's it," I encouraged her. She sucked eagerly. She needed the reassurance she was doing it right. "Suck it, baby. It feels so damn good."

She sucked even more vigorously. With more energy. When the swollen head of my cock hit the back of her throat and she gagged, I grabbed her head and groaned. I hadn't even asked for it and she'd known.

"Oh yeah. That's it. Take it all. Make me come."

My words made her suck harder and seemed to spur her on. The tighter and quicker her mouth moved, the more I had to restrain myself. Images of me shooting my load all over that pretty mouth and face made me leak. I was ready for it. To see my come dripping from her chin.

"Yeah, fuck, that's good. Fuck, baby. Suck my dick." Words were coming from my mouth without my even realizing what I said. I was lost in the sensation. My hands fisted in her hair and I began pumping into her mouth.

"Hot little mouth. Fucking owns me. Take my dick. I'm gonna come until you gag on it." The words sounded hard as I said them. My pounding pulse and the way she sucked wilder, clamping down harder with each nasty thing I said made me worse.

"Take it. Take that dick. Give it to me. That's it sweetheart. Suck it."

And she did. Harder, faster. Hungrier than any woman I had ever seen.

"AH! Beulah! I'm coming! I am fucking coming!" I cried out in case she needed to move. She didn't. Her hand stayed on my shaft as she pumped the head into her mouth even faster.

My first shot went directly into her mouth. The vision made me lose all other thought. I began growling for her to take it and slamming into her mouth. My legs felt weak as I shook from the euphoria.

When my vision began to clear, I saw the come I'd shot all over her face. Dripping off her chin. Her eyes were wide with wonder as she gazed up at me. If anything deserved to be saved this image did. It was the most erotic thing I'd ever seen.

Her tongue slipped out and she licked at the come still clinging to her lips. I trembled as I watched her. "Fuck me," I whispered.

"I'd like to. But first we both need a shower." Her tone was teasing but I knew I'd be fucking her soon. She wanted it. I wanted it. I always wanted it. This, however, just became a very close second.

"Thank you," I said not knowing the right words to say. I'd never discussed this with another woman after.

"For what exactly?"

Grinning I pulled my pants up then reached for her hands and helped her stand. "For sucking my cock like a fucking pro dressed like an angel."

She wiped the come from her chin. "Was that the polite way of saying I sucked you like a prostitute?"

I hesitated then nodded.

She laughed.

I tugged her against me. "You've ruined me," I whispered against her head.

"How?"

"I want you with me all the time. You're all I think about. I love Gerry and I'd do anything for her, but I'm jealous of her because she has you all day. How fucked up is that?"

Beulah leaned and curled into me. "You may not always feel this way. This . . . this frenzy . . . It can't always last. Can it?"

I wasn't sure. I hoped so but then again how could I function normally if it did. I answered in a way I knew I was telling the complete truth.

"I'll always be intoxicated by the sight of you."

She pulled back and stared up at me. She said nothing for a

moment. I waited for her to think about my words and I wondered myself when such poetic shit had started coming to me so easily.

"You're my fate, Stone." She repeated my words back to me. And I understood what she was saying. This was more. More than we had the words to express.

Chapter Twenty-Nine
BEULAH

STONE HAD LEFT before me this morning. Geraldine had a doctor's appointment and Stone said he needed to take her. Geraldine didn't go to her appointments willingly and if her sanity snapped while there, she was even more difficult. He didn't want me dealing with it. I had argued that I could handle it but he wouldn't listen.

He had told me to sleep in and eat breakfast. I would head over to her house at nine. They wouldn't be back until eleven but I could get started on my daily chores. I thought I should have gone with them to the doctor so I could see what to expect and learn how to deal with her. Stone couldn't always take her. I needed to be able to do it.

Arguing with Stone was pointless. I let it go. Sleeping an hour later was nice. The morning sun was bright as I stepped outside. I looked forward to the feel of fall air. We still had a while before that happened though.

Squinting against the sun it took me a moment to realize that the woman stepping out of the silver Mercedes was Portia. After that registered with me, panic quickly set in. Stone was gone. What did she want? How did she know where I was? What if this was about Heidi?

Her lifestyle hadn't changed. The white tennis outfit she was wearing said as much. She was headed to the club for tennis. Jasper had left her as she had been. Even after knowing what she'd done. There had been no consequences. He'd taken nothing from her.

"Don't look so surprised to see me. The world Stone and I circulate in talks. I've known where you were since day one. Without Jasper telling me." Her tone was haute. As if talking to me was a waste of her time.

"Why are you here?" I asked as anger began to take the place of anxiety.

"To discuss my son," she replied with annoyance. "He left Savanah, and although that is a relief, he's also so angry with me for the truths I protected him from that he won't speak to me. He won't accept my phone calls. He blames me for this." She waved her hand at the building behind me. "You're living with Stone is my fault. Losing you is all my fault. So I am being punished."

"If he's not speaking to you it's because you gave his sister away and lied about it." The disgust I felt was clear in my words.

She slid her sunglasses to the top of her head so that I had to look at her eyes. The slight roll of them made me want to slap her. "We both know Pam was a better mother. Don't act as if I did that child an injustice. I gave her a much better life than she would have had with me. As for Jasper, he's not that deep. If you fell for that, you're even more naïve than I thought. He is angry because he lost you. Like a kid who had his toy taken away."

There was no remorse. Nothing. Seeing her so unattached to a child she gave away was horrible. She had no idea the beauty she'd missed by not knowing Heidi. I was thankful she didn't want to take her from me. I didn't want Heidi in that world. This woman was evil.

"You're right. Our mother was the best. Heidi was given the love she deserved and we were blessed with the joy she brings to life. And everyone around her. You'll never know that though. How precious and wonderful she is."

Portia shifted her stance impatiently. "I've heard you sing her praises enough. I get it. You're exactly like my sister. I'm not here to discuss that. I'm here to talk about Jasper. He isn't going to forgive me until you talk to him. You need to give him a reason not to hate me. You're cousins. Yes. But maybe I was harsh. There's no need for anyone to know that. Two hundred years ago cousins were expected to marry. It wasn't incest."

I stood there in horror as she tried to make Jasper and I falling in love sound okay. Did she think I had been waiting on her approval? Shaking my head, I walked past her toward my car. I had no reason to stand here and talk to this woman. She was insane. She had no right to talk to me.

"You think you know it all. You don't. There are things you don't know. Secrets Stone knows and hasn't told you," she called out after me.

I paused. More lies. I was so tired of the lies.

"I know enough to stay away from you. That's what I know."

The nasty smirk on her face was almost intimidating. "You'll regret this."

I jerked open the car door. "All I regret is spending any time this morning listening to you spit out more lies. You're selfish

Portia. If life isn't what you want, you manipulate it until it is."

That seemed to hit a mark. Her eyes flared with anger. She didn't want to hear the truth. Someone who couldn't speak the truth wouldn't want to hear it.

"One day, you'll wish you'd listened to me."

The words meant nothing to me. She meant nothing to me. She was my mother's sister. She'd given life to my sister. But she was an empty heartless being I wanted nothing to do with her. The help she'd given me was out of guilt. It hadn't meant she had a heart. She'd been covering a lie. One that had come out. One she still hid from her world.

"He'll contact you soon. Then you'll know." Her warning was the last thing I would hear from the woman. I was getting away from her.

I climbed into my car and closed the door leaving her there. Jasper must have cut her off financially. She'd been desperate enough to come here to see me. He must be doing something to make her life difficult. I felt better about that. Jasper was a good man. I believed that. I didn't want to be disappointed in him. He was stronger than his mother.

As I pulled out of the gate, I glanced in my rearview mirror to see Portia getting back into her car. I'd have to tell Stone about this. He wouldn't like it. I didn't want to upset him but I wasn't going to keep any secrets from him either.

My phone dinged with a new text message. I was driving and didn't take it from my purse to check. Whatever it was could wait. Hopefully it wasn't Stone and I wasn't late.

Heading into the traffic I fought against thinking about all the things Portia had said. Trying to understand them was ridiculous. She was a crazed alcoholic who wasn't getting what she wanted.

Good for Jasper. It was time he stood up to her.

My phone began to ring and I ignored it again. I would check it when I was stopped in Geraldine's driveway.

Two more messages later, I pulled through the gate and came to a stop to check my phone. I never got that many messages.

Three texts from Jasper and a missed call.

The text messages started with, *We need to talk.*

Then, *Please answer my call.*

And the last, *Beulah I'll come back to see you if you don't answer me.*

I read all three texts twice before putting my phone in my purse. I continued up the driveway until I was parked in front of the house.

My stomach roiled. Dread weighed heavily on my chest.

Lies. So many lies. I didn't want to hear them. I wanted to close that door and move on with the happiness I'd found with Stone. My brief time with Jasper was jaded now with the truth. I couldn't get jerked back to that again. I wanted it over.

Another text came through. *This is important. You are and will always be the most important thing in my life.*

I couldn't bring myself to face whatever this was now. I silenced my phone and got out of the car to head inside. I had work to do. I had Stone's arms to feel safe in. I would fight for this. My world I'd found through so much pain. It had led me to more than I imagined.

Chapter Thirty
STONE

BEULAH'S EYES WERE so damn expressive. I knew the moment I walked into Gerry's house that something was wrong. Even when she smiled sweetly at me. The haunted look was there. She was hiding something.

I waited until Gerry went upstairs to take a nap from her early morning outing. I wasn't leaving without talking to Beulah. She had something to tell me. When Gerry was gone, Beulah made herself busy cleaning the kitchen and didn't make eye contact with me. I studied her waiting to see if she'd tell me what was wrong or if she'd continue to clean nervously.

The cleaning continued. After a few minutes, she glanced up at me. "Can I make you some lunch?"

"No," I replied.

She was nervous. Anxious even. But she wasn't talking. I was going to have to push harder. "Beulah," I said.

She tensed. Preparing herself.

"What is it?" I asked.

She bit her bottom lip as her eyes stayed on me. "Portia came to the apartment this morning."

Portia? What the fuck did she want? "Why?" I asked.

She shrugged. "I didn't give her time to really explain, but what I did hear was she wanted me to talk to Jasper. He's making her life difficult from what I gathered."

It hadn't been about Heidi. When I had spoken to Jasper I had been very clear about the repercussions that would follow if either he or Portia pursued the DNA test with Heidi. He had backed down. It wasn't that I didn't want him to know his sister if that was his true intention. If he'd been sincere I would have helped him work through it with Beulah so that she was secure. But when I had told him that this wasn't going to bring him closer to Beulah and that he'd be putting more of a wall between them than was already there, he had immediately backed down. He admitted that he missed Beulah. He wanted to be a part of her life. He never mentioned Heidi again.

Jasper was a good guy. I knew that more than anyone. But I also knew he was weak. He had a tendency to act impulsively and regretted his choices later. And when things were tough, he ran. Just like he'd done when his father passed away. He'd returned to Savannah this summer to take responsibility of the empire that was left to him. He needed direction. He relied on me for advice.

Beulah had changed that. He'd decided to leave Savannah without asking me. It was his first move on his own. However, it was also a way of running. I had been waiting for it. Knowing he'd stop fighting for her. It wasn't his nature.

"Do you want to talk to Jasper?" I asked. Beulah was her own woman. Although I didn't see a reason she should talk to Jasper I wouldn't be keeping her from it if she wanted to.

"No. We have nothing more to say. We had our closure."

I agreed. But the Van Allan closet wasn't empty just yet. I didn't know what exactly was still hiding in there but I knew it was there. Lurking. Waiting.

"Do you want me to handle this?"

She shook her head. "No. Just let it go away on its own. There is no reason to cause drama. I don't want you to lose your friendship with Jasper over me."

I had already lost it. Mostly. I didn't tell her that though. Losing what I had with Jasper was worth having Beulah by my side. For the first time in my life I was happy. I was complete.

"I can at least make sure Portia doesn't get on the property again. I'm sorry that happened."

"You don't have to apologize. She surprised me. She's desperate."

She was a self-serving bitch. But I didn't have to say it. Beulah knew. Reminding her that the woman who gave birth to her sister was a horrible person was pointless.

I wasn't ready to leave Beulah alone yet. I wanted to stay here and watch her relax. Her shoulders hadn't eased. She was still upset.

"Sit down, Beulah," I told her as I walked over to where she stood. She tuned to me and I pulled her in my arms and kissed her softly on the lips. "Sit down. I'm making us lunch. I'll make enough for Gerry too. She can have it when she gets up."

Beulah frowned. "That's my job."

"Don't care. Sit please. Relax."

She sighed as she walked over to take a seat at the table. "What are you making?"

I wasn't sure yet. "Depends on what is in the fridge."

"I can look in the pantry," she replied.

That caused me to smirk in memory. "You head into that pantry and I'm following you inside."

Her cheeks turned pink immediately as she smiled.

"Would that make you relax?" I asked her. Wondering if she wanted it. I'd thought after Geraldine busted us last time I'd never convince her to do it again.

She lifted one shoulder. It was shy move. Damn.

"Get in the pantry Beulah and pull your bottoms down to your ankles. Then bend over with your hands on the wall." As I said it my dick began to stiffen.

She didn't pretend to be embarrassed. Instead, she moved quickly to the pantry. Fuck. I gave her enough time to get in the exact position I wanted her in. On my way inside I found the light switch and illuminated the dark room before closing the door.

I turned to see Beulah's bare ass up in the air and her head turned to look back at me. She stood bent at the waist. Her legs far apart and a clear view of her pussy and tiny ass hole.

I kept my eyes on the area as I unzipped my jeans and pulled my dick out to begin rubbing it as I looked at her. Standing behind her, I continued slowly pumping myself and enjoyed the sight of her. She dropped her head and moaned. "Please, Stone."

Reaching a hand between her legs I found her already slick and ready. I played with her a moment and enjoyed the sounds of pleasure coming from her as her bottom wiggled. "You want to be fucked?" I asked as if it wasn't obvious.

"You know I do," she said breathlessly.

I grabbed her hips and eased in slowly. Enjoying the feel of her tight entrance sucking me in. Squeezing me. She began to move back against me anxious for me to bring her to a release.

I wasn't hurrying this. She wouldn't admit it, but she liked the idea of being caught.

"Stone, she won't sleep very much longer. Hurry," her voice was pleading.

I continued to stroke in and out of her. Easy, slow, as if we had all the time in the world.

"You worried she'll hear you getting fucked? Or are you worried you won't get to come?"

"AH! Both." She was louder this time.

I pulled out of her and went down on my knees. Just before she could beg me to get back inside I covered her needy pussy with my mouth.

"Oh God!" she cried and I smiled as her knees buckled. I licked between the folds then bit down hard on her inner thigh.

"OH,OH,OH!" She was bouncing on my face now. I began flicking her clit with my tongue and she jerked hard then went back to bouncing and moaning. She'd forgotten where we were. Her cries weren't muffled.

"Oh yes, there, like that. Just, there, AH!" she was bucking wildly. Slapping my face and tongue with her hot wet vagina. All shyness was gone. Her modesty vanished. I pulled her swollen clit into my mouth and sucked. That was her breaking point.

I had to hold both her legs as the gave out and she cried my name. Her body quivered above me. Picking her up, I turned her and picked her up. I sat her on my ready to explode dick. It slid in so quickly that she screamed and I had to cover her mouth with my own to muffle it.

I lifted her up and down on my shaft while she panted my name. Her body was still trembling. Her eyes still lost in the erotic sensation. Pressing her back against the wall I slammed into her harder and lifted her knees to just underneath my armpits. My eyes locked on hers as I saw hers glaze when she shattered yet again.

"STONE! I'm coming again." She held onto me tightly and I shot my release inside her. We were supposed to be careful waiting for her doctor's appointment. But I needed to feel this. "YES! It feels so good!"

"That's right. Take my seed baby," I said hoarsely as I held her against me jerking with each shot of pleasure.

I wanted forever.

Chapter Thirty-One
BEULAH

I HADN'T TOLD him about Jasper's text messages. I should have. I don't know why I didn't. I'd been thinking about how to tell him and didn't know if it would hinder rather than be positive. Then Stone had said he was going to fuck me in the pantry and that sounded better. It would be us joined. Close. I would be reassured he was there. With me. In me. No worry of Jasper or Portia. No concern of losing what all I'd found.

My doctor's appointment wasn't until Friday and he'd come inside me again. That was three times now. Three times he had taken a chance. I wasn't scared and I didn't regret it. When he released in me I felt marked by him. It was a hedonistic feeling and it always pushed me further into my own release. The explosion was so beautiful I forgot everything around me.

Luckily, Geraldine had slept another hour after our pantry session and when she finally came downstairs, we had already eaten chicken salad sandwiches and Stone had left. But at that moment, I hadn't cared if the Pope walked in and caught us. As long as Stone kept making my world spin.

My panties were damp. They had been all day reminding me of what we'd done. I had been able too focused on that and not Jasper. But now that I was home and Stone was here, I had to tell him. I didn't want him to think I had been hiding anything from him. I had been, but simply because I was worried about how it would affect his relationship with Jasper. Also, I didn't want to talk to Jasper.

Climbing out of my car, I walked toward the door passing the spot where Portia had stood this morning. She had been warning me that I didn't know the truth but I couldn't expect the truth from her. She was the last person I would believe. I needed to tell Stone about that too.

Inside the building it was quiet on the bottom floor. I'd seen two cars I didn't recognize outside. Someone had company and it didn't sound like Mack and Marty. Although both their vehicles were in the parking lot.

On the second floor, things were equally quiet. I was about to go up the stairs to Stone's floor when the door to Fiona's apartment opened. She stepped out into the hallway and her eyes on me immediately. She looked like gorgeous like the last time I saw. Runway model ready.

"I don't like most people," she began. "People annoy me in general. But you, I like. You're the least annoying person I've ever met. And you got rid of Presley. "

"Uh, thank you," I replied feeling awkward. This was a strange but very nice conversation. I was glad I didn't annoy her although we hardly knew each other, so I wasn't sure I could even if I tried.

"See that. Very southern and kind. Not chatty and shit.

Anyway. Because I like you I wanted to warn you. His mother is up there with the bride she's chosen for him. I've had the pleasure of meeting both crazy bitches more than once. You're welcome to come in here and stay with us if you want. He'll get rid of them soon enough."

Stone's mother was here with the fiancé he didn't acknowledge? I glanced up the stairs. I'd heard of Margot. Jasper had teased him with her, and Presley had mentioned her in anger.

"He didn't call or text me to tell me not to come. I don't know if I should hide out or if he wants me to come up there," I said my thoughts out loud.

"Who gives a fuck what he wants? Those two are vipers. They'll eat you alive."

I had the feeling Fiona didn't do relationships. She seemed more of a take care of herself and not worry about the world kind of girl. Taking her advice probably wasn't the best idea.

"He may be counting on my showing up to save him."

Fiona rolled her eyes. "God, I swear you have lived a sheltered life. I'm telling you that you can't save him. He'll need to save you."

Feminine laughter drifted down the stairs. It didn't sound like things were going badly inside. "I may come back if that's okay. I think I should go upstairs and say hello since he didn't send me a message saying otherwise."

Fiona shrugged. "I'll leave the door unlocked. Knock and come on in. I'll be on the balcony and may not hear you."

"Thank you," I told her.

"Good luck," she replied.

I smiled and she closed the door. With a deep breath that did little to calm me, I headed up the stairs and didn't stop again until I was at the apartment door. I listened. I heard a female laugh again. There was another voice too but not as loud. This was his mother. He had spoken about her, but didn't much care for her. She was still his mother and I needed to make a good impression. Glancing down at my clothes I winced. Not exactly how I would like to look meeting her the first time.

Before I opened the door, I checked my phone one more time to see if he'd messaged me. Nothing. He was expecting me. I opened the door slowly and went inside.

The voices were in the main room straight ahead. There was a tall woman standing there with dark hair that was perfectly styled and a dress that was both summery yet elegant. The heels she had on her feet however looked extremely painful. I had paused before closing the door behind me to decide who she was. Her head turned and the resemblance to Stone was unmistakable. Although she looked far too young to have a child his age.

"Who is that?" she asked as she looked at me. There was no frown but I realized that the displeasure in her eyes meant she would be frowning if she could. Her face was tight. Not much movement. She'd had work done. Maybe she was old enough to have a son Stone's age.

Stone appeared and he moved with quick long strides until he reached me. His scowl and the tension rolling off his body was enough for me to know he hadn't expected them and he didn't want them here.

"Who?" another female voice asked. The woman who I could only assume was Margot stepped into view. I didn't get a good look at her before Stone blocked my line of vision.

"Did you not get my message?" he asked.

I shook my head.

He put his hand on my shoulder. "I texted you two hours

ago to stay at Geraldine's until I called you"

I shook my head again. "I have nothing."

He sighed and ran a hand through his hair. "You don't want to be here. I'm trying to get them to leave."

"I can go stay with Fiona," I told him wishing I had.

He studied me a moment as if he was trying to make up his mind. "It's not that I don't want you here. It's that they are vicious. I prefer to keep you far away from them."

"Is that Margot?" I whispered.

He frowned. "Yes. How do you know about her?"

"Jasper, Presley. Your supposed fiancé has been mentioned a few times." I was trying to make a joke but the scowl on his face made it obvious he wasn't amused.

"Winston, who is this girl that walked right into your apartment without knocking. Please tell me it's the help and not another child of your father's ex-wives." His mother sounded amused with her last remark. Margot giggled.

"Fuck them," he muttered then turned around to face them with his hand splayed possessively on my back. "Mother, Margot, this is Beulah Edwards. She's my girlfriend and she lives here."

If he'd slapped his mother and kicked her in the gut her expression could not have been more horrified. She even paled. Several shades actually.

Margot let out a sharp laugh. I looked at her then. She was petite, beautiful, stunning even, and polished. Dark blonde hair that was silky and straight with blue eyes that reminded me of a swimming pool. The pink full lips seemed almost unnatural. "You can't be serious," his mother said.

His hand gripped my waist this time and pressed my body tightly up against his own. "You'll check your words, mother. Or you'll leave my home."

"This isn't your home. Manhattan is your home," Margot drawled as if this was all very amusing.

"And you're not my mother. Nor are you family. I have no reason to issue you even a shred of hospitality. You can leave now."

Margot's amused look turned to one of shock. Her eyes widened and she did a very good imitation of someone who had been offended.

"Winston! You will not talk to her that way. Margot is practically your fiancé. How do you think this makes her feel?"

"For the love of God woman, I have NEVER once acted like I was remotely interested in Margot romantically. Just because you decided I would marry her when I was ten does not constitute a fucking engagement. Both of you are delusional."

Margot walked regally toward the door where we were standing, briefly stopping just to the right of Stone. If eyes could cut someone, her glance could have sliced you open. "I won't be waiting on you. I will move on."

"Thank you," his replay was one of relief.

She walked out not waiting for his mother. A lot less dramatic than Presley had been.

"You're letting her walk out?" his mother asked throwing her hand in the direction of the door.

"I'm hoping you will follow suite," he drawled.

She threw her angry glare at me. "He'll bore of you. It takes proper breeding and a brain to intrigue and challenge him." She then stalked past us not looking at her son again.

When she was gone, he closed the door and locked it. His shoulders sagged and he hung his head. I worried for a moment that he regretted sending them away.

"Why can't I have a mother who wants nothing more than to see me. Or simply call and check on me. Not bring her agendas to shove down my throat? My father has the worst taste in women." He turned and looked at me. "I'm sorry you walked in on that. I tried to save you from it."

"I thought I wanted to meet your mother. She's your family after all. I was wrong. But I am even more thankful for Geraldine than I was before."

He smiled at the sound of her name. "Why are you thankful for Gerry?"

"Because she loved the little boy who needed it."

A softness touched his eyes and he held out a hand to me. "Come here."

I walked into his arms willingly and sighed with contentment as we stood there in the silence.

His mother, Portia, Jasper, Margot—none of them matter. Just this. Just us.

Chapter Thirty-Two
JASPER

SECRETS WERE LIES in their own right. One couldn't keep a secret without a lie. And we revered someone who could keep a secret, yet scorned those who lied. It was the same. They all melded together.

Stone had been my brother since we were kids. Both raised by parents who neglected us. He was beaten regularly by his father while mine never laid a hand on me. Other than that, we were the same. We existed in the same world. He was expected to run a company he was to inherit. To carry on an empire that had never been his dream. Marry well. It didn't matter if we didn't love our wives. We'd be expected to have affairs. This was our world.

It had been. It's what I had finally accepted. Then Beulah had walked into my world and changed me. She made me want something real. Gave me a reason to smile. Parties meant to entertain me were no longer needed. The lost boy had been found.

Immediately after I had found her and knew I loved her, she

was taken so permanently leaving me with nothing. No hope. No chance at a future with her in it. Not even as a friend. It had ended abruptly.

Glancing up at the building in front of me I felt guilt for this. Stone's secrets had always been like my own. I'd take them to the grave. But he'd stolen her so easily. Without guilt or remorse. He'd facilitated the end of all contact I had with her. My fucking shattered heart was of no consequence to him. He'd said he was protecting her.

From me? I adored her. I would stand in front of a motherfucking bullet for the woman. I didn't care that we were related. I would have moved away with her. Changed my name and given up fortune if I could have her by my side. The blood in our veins didn't make me love her less. Nothing ever would.

She thought she knew Stone. She thought she was in love with him. Stone had his own set of secrets. A past that made him not worthy of Beulah. He hated his father but he had reason. However, that hate had sent him spiraling out of control many times over the years and he'd let his father clean it up. He wasn't the man Beulah believed him to be. He'd exposed the secrets that would keep her from me. I was only returning the favor.

The pictures in my hand felt heavy with regret. I had fought doing this for weeks, not wanting to expose him. Even after he'd taken Beulah. I didn't want to do it but I would because she deserved to know. She needed to know.

The walk up the stairs to his apartment was a blur as I battled internally. She'd never be mine. I knew that. Our bloodlines would keep her from ever accepting us. But she wouldn't stay here with him after she knew. If I couldn't have her then she should be with someone worthy of her. Stone was stable now. He hadn't acted out to spite his father in a couple years. But his past was there. It would be back to haunt him. He knew it just as well as I did.

I rang the bell and waited. He wasn't here yet. There would only be the short amount of time I had to show her. The worst at least. Many of his transgressions were that of a wealthy, damaged kid. But there was one. One that was a secret she wouldn't be able to forgive him for.

The door opened slowly and Beulah stood there staring at me nervously. She'd had to know it was me before she opened the door and she'd opened it anyway. She trusted me. She didn't want to, but she knew I was innocent of my parents' deceit.

"I need to show you something," I told her.

"What?" she asked her voice shaky. She hadn't sent me away. She wanted to know.

"This," I handed her the photos. They were the most damaging. Without words, she would be able to tell who it was. What she didn't know. But the explanation as to where that little boy was now would be unforgivable. I knew her well enough to know she wouldn't be able to accept it. Or understand it. I did. I wasn't sure I wouldn't have done the same at sixteen.

Stone had come into her life because of me. He had exposed lies I hadn't even known and then taken her from me. I was only being fair and I had done nothing wrong. My morals weren't in question. Stone's would be.

"What is this?" she shook her head looking at the photos.

"You can look at him and tell who it is," I replied.

She paled. Lifted her eyes to meet mine. "No. I don't believe you."

But she did. I saw the doubt there. "Ask him, Beulah. See what he says."

She looked at the photos in her hand. "No. This, it isn't real. Why are you doing this? Why would you show this to me?"

I started to explain more when the door at the entrance of the building slammed shut and the ground shook from its force. He was home. He knew I was here. He'd seen my car. This was the beginning of their end. Soon she'd be gone. Free to start a life without our darkness and lies. The sweet little lies he'd told her would all go up in smoke. After all, how could she forgive a man who ignores his own son and allows the boy to grow up with the same monster of a father he did?

ABBI GLINES

ABBI GLINES IS a #1 New York Times, USA Today, and Wall Street Journal bestselling author of the Rosemary Beach, Sea Breeze, Vincent Boys, Existence, and The Field Party Series . She never cooks unless baking during the Christmas holiday counts. She believes in ghosts and has a habit of asking people if their house is haunted before she goes in it. She drinks afternoon tea because she wants to be British but alas she was born in Alabama. When asked how many books she has written she has to stop and count on her fingers. When she's not locked away writing, she is reading, shopping (major shoe and purse addiction), sneaking off to the movies alone, and listening to the drama in her teenagers lives while making mental notes on the good stuff to use later. Don't judge.

You can connect with Abbi online in several different ways. She uses social media to procrastinate.

www.abbiglines.com
www.facebook.com/abbiglinesauthor
twitter.com/AbbiGlines
www.instagram.com/abbiglines
www.pinterest.com/abbiglines

books by ABBI GLINES

As She Fades

ROSEMARY BEACH SERIES
Fallen Too Far
Never Too Far
Forever Too Far
Rush Too Far
Twisted Perfection
Simple Perfection
Take A Chance
One More Chance
You We're Mine
Kiro's Emily
When I'm Gone
When You're Back
The Best Goodbye
Up In Flames

SEA BREEZE SERIES
Breathe
Because of Low
While It Lasts
Just For Now
Sometimes It Lasts
Misbehaving
Bad For You
Hold On Tight
Until The End

SEA BREEZE MEETS ROSEMARY BEACH
Like A Memory
Because of Lila

THE FIELD PARTY SERIES
Until Friday Night
Under the Lights
After the Game

ONCE SHE DREAMED
Once She Dreamed (Part 1)
Once She Dreamed (Part 2)

THE VINCENT BOYS SERIES
The Vincent Boys
The Vincent Brothers

THE MASON DIXON SERIES
Boys South of the Mason Dixon
Brothers South of the Mason Dixon

THE SWEET SERIES
Sweet Little Thing
Sweet Little Lies
Sweet Little Memories

EXISTENCE TRILOGY
Existence (Book 1)
Predestined (Book 2)
Leif (Book 2.5)
Ceaseless (Book 3)

Made in the USA
Lexington, KY
24 August 2018